STRANGERS

Strangers

Stories

Rebecca Ruth Gould

Cover art: "Man and Woman on Bench" Juan Gris, 1908/09

Cover design by Jacob Arms
Paperback ISBN: 9781947175839

Published by Serving House Books
Lawrence Landing Company
Raleigh, North Carolina 27609
United States of America
www.servinghousebooks.com

Serving House Books is a proud member of

Independent Book Publishers Association
 and
Community of Literary Magazines and Presses

CONTENTS

To migrants—

> *whose homes move*
>> *against their yearning*
>>> *for stasis—*
>>>> *everywhere.*

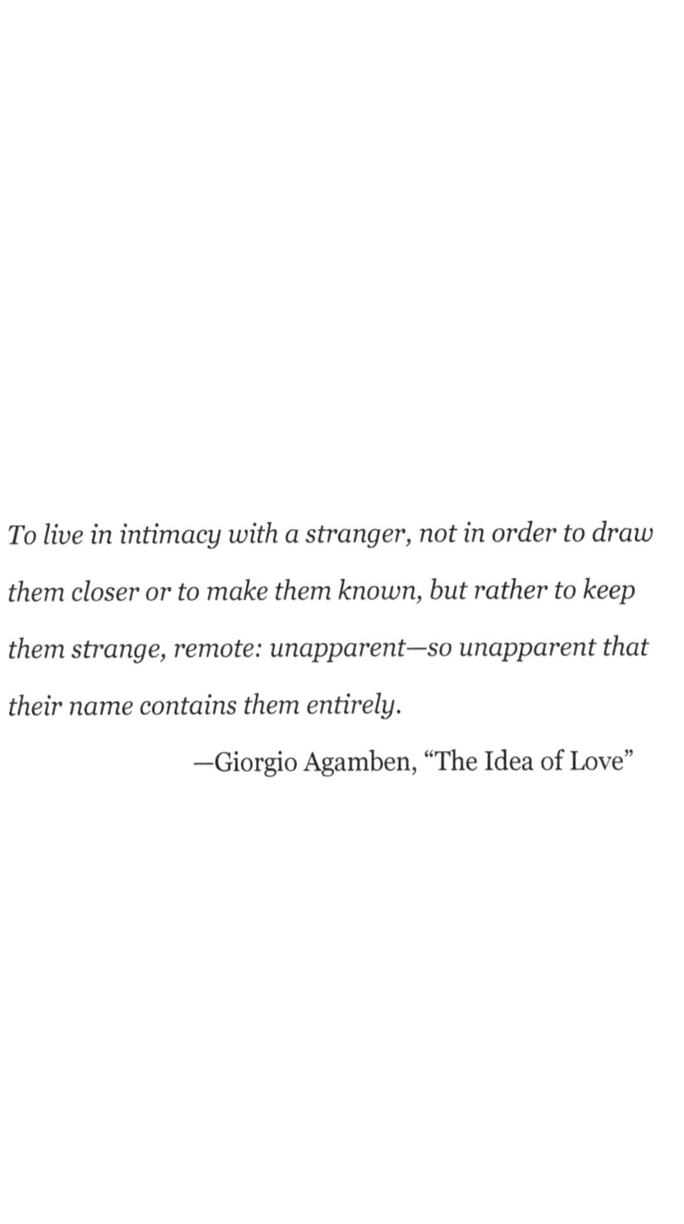

To live in intimacy with a stranger, not in order to draw them closer or to make them known, but rather to keep them strange, remote: unapparent—so unapparent that their name contains them entirely.

—Giorgio Agamben, "The Idea of Love"

OF PLACES AND PEOPLE:
ON WRITING *STRANGERS*

The writing of the stories that comprise *Strangers* extends across more than a decade. It was only towards the end of the process, after I had completed three of the stories, that I realized how much they had in common with each other. Like a compulsion, the same story kept repeating itself, albeit with significant variations and in different locations. These stories are about lost bonds, fleeting connections, and relationships formed at a distance, based on minimal knowledge of the other, yet occasionally yielding deep insights into their soul. They are about love as projection, and love's impossibility, as well as its utter centrality to all that makes life worthwhile.

The geography in which these stories transpire matters too and is inseparable from the relations that evolve among the characters. My initial aim was to record my impressions of the cities that had etched themselves into my life. Tbilisi, Damascus, Budapest, New York City, London, Bristol. The nonfiction medium that had served me well in documenting everyday life in the Caucasus and the Middle East, from the war zones of Chechnya to the debates around the hijab in the Islamic Republic of Iran, was coming up short when it came to traversing more intimate spaces.[1]

---

[1] For such nonfictional writings, see Rebecca Ruth Gould, *Writers and Rebels: The Literature of Insurgency in the Caucasus* (New Haven: Yale University Press, 2016) and Rebecca Ruth Gould, "Hijab as Commodity Form: Veiling, Unveiling, and Misveiling in Contemporary Iran," *Feminist Theory* 15(3): 221-240.

These undocumented spaces contained the stories of lives lived beneath what Anton Chekhov described in his short story "Lady with a Lapdog" as "the important, fascinating, and real" life that takes place "under the cover of a secret, as if under the cover of night." Chekhov was writing about a male protagonist, Gurov, who encounters a woman on a park bench, much as in Juan Gris's painting, "Man and Woman on Bench." He can be forgiven for centring a male perspective concerning what happens under the cover of night. While Gurov's double life is relatable, it follows a pattern that differs from the inner lives of most of the women I have known. More needed to be said from a woman's perspective about the secret life that passes under the cover of night, and sometimes in broad daylight.

Not every city through which my life has passed has found its way into these stories, but every city named in these stories has haunted my waking and asleep hours. I lived in Berlin for the better part of a year, yet I found that the city was more suited for poetry.[2] Similarly, I lived in Bethlehem, in Occupied Palestine, yet I have only been able to write about my experiences there in nonfiction and poetry.[3]

Though I am US-born, I have found it difficult to write about the country of my birth. New York City is the only American setting for my stories. As for the decade and a half that I passed in American suburbia during my childhood and adolescence, my muse deserts me whenever

---

[2] These poems found their way into my first poetry collection, *Cityscapes* (Monee, IL: Alien Buddha Press, 2019).
[3] See Rebecca Ruth Gould, *Erasing Palestine: Free Speech and Palestinian Freedom* (London and New York: Verso Books, 2023).

I attempt to render it in literary form. My year in Singapore was similarly glossed over in unwilling silence. Although *Strangers* gathers together stories I have carried within me for over a decade, this book does not comprise an autobiography and cannot be reduced to the story of my life. Rather, they are callings from every place that has found its way into these fictions, and into my life. Much is entirely invented, but everything was *felt* in the particular way these words record.

"One does not love a place the less for having suffered in it," Anne Elliot in Jane Austen's novel *Persuasion* presciently observes. Similarly, one does not love a place more for having been happy there. The emotions and experiences that I have channelled in these stories lie beyond happiness and sorrow. I wanted to capture in time that bedrock sense of affiliation, that tethered and sometimes desperate clasp to specific buildings, homes, streets, and spaces, that anchors our soul amid all that life brings us. These places and spaces provide an elusive continuity to the uncertainty of existence. For much of my life, the streets along which I roamed have been the medium for my muse. When I could not speak, I could nonetheless walk through dimly lit streets, and along sparsely populated embankments. I often walked, late at night. No matter how lost I was, I could always speak to the waters that wound silently through whatever city I happened to reside in: Budapest's Danube, London's Thames, New York City's Hudson, Tbilisi's Mtkvari, or Bristol's Avon. These waterways—along with the bridges that covered them—are the mediums through which many of the characters in this collection were first conceived.

Having invoked my life, a word needs to be said about

my own relationship to the characters who populate these fictions. Readers will ask: Who is Teresa? Is she the author in fictional guise? While the total collapse of the author's voice into her characters' voices defeats the purpose of literary fiction, too much distance causes the stories she creates to fall flat. Both must be avoided at all costs.

My own favoriteauthors navigate the author-character relationship with extreme empathy and vulnerability, as I have aimed to do in these pages. They do not fear identifying with the offspring of their imagination. Even in a novel such as *Madame Bovary,* which is famous for introducing the aesthetic of the invisible author into world literature, the author's love for Emma is evident to any careful reader. "Emma is myself," declared Flaubert of his famed heroine, with whom his narrative voice never identified or merged.

As her creator, I know Teresa well. I relate to her as if she were myself. The *as if* is crucial, though, for she is not me. I understand what drove Teresa far from her native land to Tbilisi and Damascus, as well as what drove her away from her temporary homes. But Teresa is ultimately a stranger to me, a character with whom I have only a fleeting connection, like many characters that pass through her life in these stories.

Teresa does not appear in all of these stories. The stories with male protagonists—"Goodbye, Home" and "Like a Cavafy Poem,"—have not encountered her, yet. I could not find any place in those narratives for her ambitions or dreams. As for the male characters who move those stories forward, Jeremiah in "Goodbye, Home" and the protagonists of "Like a Cavafy Poem," they are also strangers but not for that reason any less dear.

One thing that all of the characters have in common,

and which I have in common with them as their creator and as a human being, is that they are strangers to each other, and to themselves. And this brings me to the dimension of these stories that haunts me the most and which inspired their title, *Strangers.* The strangeness we find in others, which sometimes prompts our love and at other times our hate, crucially determines our relationship to ourselves.

Everything we need to know in life can be condensed into those moments when we discover how little we know about those people whom we thought we knew best. In these revelatory moments, we discover that we know almost nothing at all, either about them, or about the world we inhabit with them. Human beings are mysteries, first and foremost to themselves. So long as we are free, so will we elude each other, as well as ourselves. In simpler words, these stories show what happens when we become strangers to ourselves.

Often, we become most acutely aware of our strangeness to each other when we fall in love. To the extent that this book is about love, it documents much more than the experience of falling in love. Many of the characters in these stories spend more time manipulating and hurting each other—and themselves—than they spend in a state of infatuation. Whether or not they find love, they perpetually seek it, and they know that those moments of mystery that we experience with the others on our journey are part of what it is to love.

Since the age of thirteen, I have been trying to make sense of the mystery of our strangeness to ourselves and to each other. Dostoevsky, Tolstoy, George Eliot, and Thomas Hardy have helped me along the way. Yet it was not enough for me to read fiction in order to probe this mystery. I also had to write fictions in which characters I loved lived through my fears and dreams. I had to stand by them as they made choices I could not approve of or comprehend, but which I had to accept and document in excruciating detail. Perhaps it is further testimony of the strangeness of our creations to ourselves that these stories were first published as a collection in Arabic by the Iraqi publisher al-Hajjan in the ancient city of Basra, thanks to the generous and persistent labours of the Syrian writer, critic, and translator Saleh Razzouk.[4]

Written in English, these stories were first shared with the world in Arabic, in a land, Iraq, that was illegally invaded and occupied by the country of my birth. Now, four years later, these fugitive fictions have returned home, to be presented to English readers in book form for the first time. But they are still—and will always be—in exile, just like their author, who has not lived in the country of her publisher for twelve years and who has no intention to ever return.

Before closing, it remains to be said that these stories were all written before 2023, although some have been revised since. 2023 marks the beginning of the US-supported genocide of the Palestinian people by Israel. Everything I write now is written under the shadow of that ongoing atrocity. "Goodbye, Home" speaks directly to Israel's dispossession of the Palestinian people, but it belongs to an earlier era. The political awakening that we see taking place in the main character, Jeremiah, is belated

---

[4] عشاق غرباء [Strangers in Love], translated by Saleh Razzouk (Basra, Iraq: al-Hajjan Press, 2021).

and insufficient, particularly in light of what is happening now. But it marks a beginning, an inaugural parting of ways with the lies spread by the imperial formations that have shaped these characters' lives.

Saying goodbye, as many of these characters do, means cultivating a new self that can reject relationship governed by imperial dynamics. While the imperial context for many of these stories is not directly dwelt on, the US empire's ubiquitous reach causes many of my characters to feel alienated and intensifies the pressure on them to seek ways to leave home.

I am grateful to the moments that writing these stories have given me, for making me understand myself and my place in the world a bit better, for helping me to see the people in my life from different angles, and for etching in my mind's eye the places where I have suffered and loved. I offer these stories to you, dear reader, in the hopes that they may help you probe the depths of your own humanity. May they cause you to look differently on strangers and to regard them as intrinsically related to yourself. May they bathe the people and places who have passed through your life and penetrated the corners of your soul in an aura of mystery, like ancient icons, speaking to us of another world.

Rebecca Ruth Gould
2 October 2025

1.

Hands

What struck her most about him were his hands. They were long and lanky, like his body. Even more remarkable than their shape was the way he used them. When they first met, he shook her hand boldly and directly, as if it were a perfectly normal thing to do and not a violation of the law in the Islamic Republic of Iran. Taken aback, she forgot to respond. Her hand hung limply in his palm, until he dislodged it.

Just the day prior, she had read about a poet who, after returning from abroad, had been arrested for shaking a woman's hand. She wanted to warn him: *You shouldn't do that. You might end up in jail.* But he must have known what he was doing, she reasoned, and who was she to tell him how to behave in his own country?

His hands didn't fit anywhere, not in his pockets, or at his sides. They dangled oddly from his arms, like an expert swimmer more at home in a lake than on dry land. The lines on his palms were long, stretching from his wrist to his index fingers. If a fortune-teller—like the one she had consulted in Hafez's tomb while visiting Shiraz—had been asked to read his palms she would have predicted for him a long life, a fulfilling marriage and many children. His hands were like an autonomous body. She imagined them keeping her warm at night, soothing the aches in her back, providing a resting ground for her lips, caressing her hips.

Before they said goodbye that magical night in Tehran in front of the Golestan Palace, she asked him why he decided to shake her hand. Without answer he waxed lyrical, in a different direction. "I dream of working wonders with my hands," he said, "I want to make magic potions and aphrodisiacs based on ancient Iranian traditions." Although it was not an answer, his words opened a new mysterious horizon onto his soul. She wanted to know more.

She touched his hands again in Tbilisi, a city they had arranged to rendezvous in order to get to know each other better. Across the border, where it was safe. Christian Iranians and Bahais walked the streets of Tbilisi openly, freely proclaiming their faith. The walls of certain homes were covered with signs in Farsi. There in the Georgian Republic, they could say things—about each other, to each other, about their lives—that could not be said so long as the morality police of the Islamic Republic was watching them. Closed circuit cameras and bugs in hotels. They could hold hands publicly, without breaking the law.

Funny, she thought, how law interacts with morality, indeed with honesty: what is licit in one country suddenly becomes an offence when the jurisdiction shifts. As if there were no universal or transcendent ethics. As if, even in the Islamic Republic, everything were just a game of power and politics. Strange how acts of affection, expressions of love, can be made into crimes.

Her hands pressed hard on his body. Certain parts of him yielded in certain ways, though not every crevice and not in every way. He was nervous and gently, tenderly, resistant. Her hands traced a continual arc on his back while they worked together to etch each other's body in their memory, to stimulate the words that flowed between them like a fresh shower on a hot summer day, summoning and cementing memory, not just for that instant, but for eternity.

She saw his hands again in Abu Dhabi, but this time it was different. This time it was she who was cautious. She wanted to see what his hands would do with her body—how he would touch her and when and why—when unprompted. Nearly all of their contact had been initiated by her hands in Tbilisi. This time, she decided, she would let his fingers determine their movements, would wait for his nails to dig into her skin, and his thumbs to press into the small of her back. She imagined her spine curve, bending into his hands. As she waited for him to touch her, the hours passing relentlessly with him making no movements, giving no sign of the love growing between them, she remembered when he shook her hands unbidden in full public view in violation of the law, in Tehran. Looking back on that moment, she wondered whether she had misread the target of his apparent defiance. Was it perhaps a performance, not for her sake, but for the state, an act of civil disobedience that dared the government to punish him?

Hospitality demands that we shake the hands of every guest, his handshake seemed to say in retrospect, as he failed to touch her. *We must show our respect to every visitor!* Or was she demeaning that miraculous moment? What force of gravity had caused him to extend his hand to her, only to withdraw it when they were finally alone?

She had never seen his hands so reticent as they were in Abu Dhabi. Neither in Tehran nor Tbilisi were they like that: tentative, passive, even cold. It was as if they belonged in another place, on another body, or in another galaxy. She decided she would wait until they said goodbye to question why his hands appeared to be tied down by a psychic force she could not fathom, why they were so hesitant to touch her body. And then, in the airport, there was a crush of people, as there always is. They were late. The lines extended out into the arrivals hall as the boarding time approached. 5:30. 5:35. 5:40. The day was just beginning, yet it felt like the end of time.

All passengers for Tehran please approach gate 6D, the intercom blared. The moment to speak had passed—she had to touch his hands. She reached out to find them, but they were tucked deep inside his pockets, too deep for her to reach.

The deferral of discussion, along with his unreachable hands that could have brought words to his lips, prevented her from asking the question that was burning on her lips: when would their hands meet again? He asked her to watch his luggage while he went to the bathroom. When he returned, he had to rush to catch his flight. There was no time to say goodbye, no time to repeat the gestures that brought them together in Tehran and Tbilisi, no time for her to take the measure of his hands, to press his knuckles on her cheek, to lift his fingertips to her lips and to tell him how much she wanted his hands—but actually the entirety of his body and of his soul—in her life. Perhaps, she decided, the crush of people was the best way of deferring this impossible speech. Maybe silence was the preferred option. Not knowing what to say in the little time remaining to them, she closed her eyes and imagined his fingers stroking her hair. When she opened her eyes, he was gone.

2.

Speaking in Tongues

Teresa moved to Damascus just after Ramadan in September 2010. She timed her arrival to coincide with the feast of Eid al-Fitr so she wouldn't feel pressured to forgo drinking water during the day out of respect for her Muslim friends. She had decided to take a break after graduating from the university and before embarking on a career. Since she didn't know what she was going to do with her life, she decided to focus on her lifelong dream: to speak Arabic. Back home in Illinois, she had tried many times, and failed. She had managed to pick up some Persian along the way, but Arabic so far had defeated her completely. Amid the monoglots of the American Midwest, all foreign languages seemed distant, and dead.

So she decided to embark on a journey, to break with her past, to create a new life for herself in an unknown world. As the home of so many great Arab writers, and of the Levantine dialect that was so close to classical Arabic poetry, Syria was the perfect destination. She rented out a room in the Salhiyeh district, one of Damascus' most traditional and religious neighborhoods, where the medieval Sufi mystic Ibn Arabi had lived. His tomb was a pilgrimage site, which she visited every day during the first week of her arrival. She also attended religious classes at the nearby Abu'l Nour mosque in hopes of improving her Arabic. After a few weeks, the lessons, which were intended for young children, became exasperating and comical. She could tell all the fairy tales and nursery rhymes she wanted to, but had no idea how to live as an adult in the language of the country where she was.

So she started asking around for someone who could give her private lessons in Arabic, and reveal to her a new dimension of this language. She finally found a retired schoolteacher who began visiting her every day, loaded down with textbooks and lesson plans. Although the lessons were exhilarating at first, eventually they bored her too. She missed the simple pleasures of aimless conversation, drinking coffee with friends, and touching the hands of a lover. That too she longed to do in Arabic. But it was impossible, with her kindergarten level of knowledge of the language. She called up Mona, a friend she had met at a local bookstore, and asked her if she could widen her network of acquaintances.

"This isn't for the sake of language learning," Teresa said, "I'm desperate for human contact. I want to talk about books, history, anything other than my Arabic lessons."

Her friend happily obliged. She called her back the next day and offered to introduce her to a PhD student at the University of Damascus.

"He's brilliant," Mona said, as if making a sales pitch. "He'll be the first Iranian to write a thesis on our great Iraqi poet Badr al-Shakir al-Sayyab."

Teresa was intrigued.

"Like you he's a migrant," Mona added, "just here temporarily. You two have a lot in common. I'm sure he'll show you the best parts of Syria."

Mona arranged a meeting for the three of them the next day at a café in Damascus's hip Sarouja district.

The first impression was unforgettable. His towering height and the radiance of his amber skin cast a spell. The only thing that made her uncomfortable were his hands, which seemed too soft, almost as if he had never experienced any struggles in life, and didn't know the meaning of work. Those hands reminded her of royalty, and of people whom she instinctively felt could not be trusted. She forced herself to forget her discomfort as soon as she became conscious of it.

Teresa had always regarded love at first sight as a cheap trick from romance novels, but now she began to wonder whether she had been wrong to dismiss the concept out of hand. There was something magical, even otherworldly, in the way he looked at her.

He introduced himself as Mehdi. "My name means savior," he explained.

"In Arabic?" she asked, though she was well aware of the word and its meaning.

"In Persian, too." He smiled. "My native tongue."

She had learned all this in her university textbook: Mehdi was the Messiah, who appears at the end of times, to rid the world of evil and injustice. Sunnis didn't believe in the Mehdi, but the man who had just captivated her was no Sunni. His angelic beauty seemed somehow feminine. Not the kind she associated with men. Not that it mattered. His strangeness was part of his appeal.

"Are you American?" he asked. She nodded yes.

He told her that he was planning to soon move to the USA. He had a job offer, he explained. He would be a lobbyist in Washington, DC. She was skeptical—how could he have landed a job like that in faraway Damascus, with substandard English to boot? Would the US authorities really give him a visa? She decided not to inquire further. Soon, she had forgotten what he had said.

They discovered within minutes what lay concealed within each other's languages, dormant until they met each other. The external world receded as they crafted a secret idiom from their native tongues. She was a native speaker of English, with some conversational Persian. He was a native speaker of Persian, with some conversational English. As soon as they were introduced in the Damascus café, they began to build bridges between their two languages, connecting their countries and cultures, testing each other's limits, and admiring the strange, exotic words that only they understood. Mona observed them with a smile. A satisfied matchmaker.

As the three of them parted, Mehdi turned to Teresa.

"Would you like to join me next Saturday?" he asked. "I'm going to the book fair." She squeezed her friend's hand, and agreed to Mehdi's proposal without thinking twice. She thought of how nice it would be to be with him alone, without anyone to mediate between them, free to invent a language that was accessible only to each other.

She passed the interval between Wednesday and Saturday immersed in her Arabic lessons, but thinking constantly of him. Ever since they parted in front of the café, the memory of his proximity filtered through her consciousness. It became a ghost, haunting her sleep. The traces of his fresh breath lingering on her shoulders electrified her, evoking his absence. She waited for Saturday by repeating the same action, as if it were a beat in a song. She would memorize a sentence in Arabic, and then press her hand against her neck, on the place where his breath had lingered. She repeated this process until her mind was filled with Arabic sounds and she could no longer absorb more words.

Saturday arrived. They met at the bus stop. As the bus wove between traffic jams, making its way to the book fair on the outskirts of the city, near the airport, their bodies rubbed gently against each other. An Anglo-Persian idiom slowly developed between them, comprised of half-sentences, knowing phrases, and mutually understood words. The more words they exchanged, the more private their language became.

By the time they arrived at the book fair, no outside listener would have been able to decipher their artificial language. When they disembarked from the bus, they shifted to a more public way of speaking, a global, all-purpose English, cleansed of any trace of their identities. He took her on a tour of his favorite bookstalls, and helped her bargain with the booksellers.

By the end of their trip, she had filled her bags, and had to buy a second bag just to carry all the books she had purchased. Most of the books she knew she would never read, because they were in languages and scripts she could not even decipher: Sorani Kurdish, a Quran printed without dots, even Syriac. She was overcome by the urge to collect texts for their own sake, when they were inscribed in beautiful and challenging scripts. She planned to display them on her bookshelves, and to touch them whenever she needed to remember that night with Mehdi, her new Iranian friend.

She returned to her apartment late that night, collapsed onto the bed, and slept like a child. The impression that he had left her with in the café had been confirmed at the book fair. She had only just arrived in Syria, and the war was months away. A distant, inscrutable future. Damascus was a haven of peace. She could walk the streets of her neighborhood at night without fear. The food was fresh, the cost of living reasonable. Her neighbors were friendly. Most importantly, Arabic was everywhere. It filled her mind and her heart, creating conditions propitious for love. For the first time in many years, she finally felt liberated from the world's burdens. And it was nice to be as far as possible from home. Still it was too early to be sure about what was happening between them. She had to wait for him to make the next move.

The days passed in waiting. Ever since she met him, her body seemed to be controlled by her attraction to him. She could as little direct its movements as she could guide the morning tide. She passed the period of his absence wondering what had happened to her friends and family back in Illinois. No one had written, though she had been in Damascus for a week. For her parents, Syria was an exotic country, far removed from the habitable world. It could just as easily have been on the moon. When she told them where she was going, it was as if they had given up on her as a person, as if she were exiling herself from the human species and they in return were severing their ties of kinship.

Why didn't they write? she wondered. *Why didn't they ask whether she had arrived safely?* The longer she waited, the more she realized that she didn't expect to hear from them. The person she was truly waiting for was Mehdi, who had captivated her ever since he showed her where all the best books were to be found at the book fair. At long last, after three days, came the call she had been waiting for.

"I just wanted to see how you are," he said softly in an accent-free English that must have been rehearsed many times before in the mirror prior to making the call. His pronunciation was perfect, though the grammar was faulty. His grammatical lapses charmed her in ways she could not begin to explicate. The more idiosyncratic his speech, the stronger her attraction. She suppressed the urge to correct his grammar, and instead replied in an equally broken idiom she knew he would understand, "I missing you so much."

They built a language together during the nights they spent together, in the coffee shops of downtown Damascus, smoking the *nargile* and sharing fresh strawberry drinks. She loved how he pronounced the rich sherberty concoction: *freeze*, felicitously conjoining the Arabic word for strawberry with the English verb. They walked hand in hand down Damascus's deserted streets, crowned by rows of grapevines hovering above their heads, trading ancient words and inventing new ones. Only on rare occasions did they converse exclusively in his native tongue, the language he identified as the one spoken by Cyrus the Great of Persia, or in her English, a language she regarded as inherently corrupt, having been spread thin across the global.

With time, they cultivated a language that only made sense to the two of them. It could not be transcribed and could only be spoken, preferably in bed, or while they were making love. Their creole tongue was a sign of the bond that was forming between them. It was the only language that could capture their mutual intimacy.

The first time he slept with her, he prefaced his proposal with his mother's advice:

"My mother told me that when I touch a woman I must be soft and gentle with her. I must clean her body before I make love to her. Would you like to go swimming?"

Teresa was perplexed by his question. It was cold outside and they had not yet dressed. "Swimming?" she repeated. "Do you have a pool?"

"*Dush, dush*," he whispered, pressing forward in the hopes that she would understand what he could not translate. She understood. He picked her up and carried her to the shower, where as promised, he cleansed her entire body, from head to foot, with the same single-minded devotion a mother brings to bathing her child. Except she could not tell who was the mother and who was the child.

Every night, he repeated in the Persian-English concoction that they called Pinglish the phrases that gave him control over her, that made her feel like she was falling in love, although, like most clichés, she did not know what that meant: *delam tang shodeh* (my heart has constricted from missing you), *dustet daram* (I love you), *damet garm* (may your breath be warm). And then the names, the many names by which they called to each other, as numerous and various as the names for God: *arus-i man* (my bride), *hasti-yi-man* (my being), *zindegi-yi-man* (my life), *dokhtar-i man* (my girlfriend), *bahr-i man* (my sea), *okeanus-i man* (my ocean), *keshvar-i man* (my country). Language became its own force of attraction, supplanting all other desires.

They played games with words. He asked how much she missed him while she searched for ever more adventurous comparisons: *chun rige biaban* (like the sands in the desert), *chun qatrehyi bahr* (like the water in the sea). When she played the game well—when she became for a brief instant more versatile in his native tongue even than he—he would wrap his fingers around hers and whisper in her ear: *to mu'jize-man hasti* (you are my miracle). Then they would talk about angels and stars and all kinds of celestial things that people do not commonly talk about in the language of their homeland. Things that she could never have shared with someone who did not share her love of speaking in tongues.

When they spoke in Persian, shame disappeared. She remembered learning once in the university that the Persian term *sharm*, in spite of its morphological link to the English "shame," had no true equivalent in any other language. The Persian social conscience was at once stronger and more oppressive than any other tongue, her teacher said. Even if that were true, she decided, there could be no shame with Mehdi.

With Mehdi, she could only be herself fully by becoming another. She told him stories about the past she was too scared to share even with her friends. Her invented Persian identity—fabricated from the words on his tongue, as if borrowed from his flesh—freed her from her American one. This was true in spite of the guttural tongue twister he challenged her to pronounce, such as *Khaqan khayli khub* (the king is very good). She knew she could never speak like a native Iranian. He understood her Persian when no one else could. She understood—indeed, she preferred—the broken English he had scraped together from Shakespeare, Hemingway, and Beatles songs.

Their shared language conjured an image of their future together. They began dreaming of marriage two weeks into their acquaintance, and of children by third.

Their fantasies were inconsistent and full of contradictions, but everything seemed possible in the utopias fashioned from their multiple tongues. Together they dreamed just for the pleasure of dreaming, without regard for the consequences. Mehdi's skillful use of language to fulfill his fantasies was a self-sustaining passion, and it infected her too. Whether his fantasies would ever be realized mattered less than the pleasure he took in uttering them in many different tongues.

Jawhar-i man (my gem), he said.

Falak-i man (my sky), she replied.

That was why she got into this trade in the first place: like Ibn Arabi, who had motivated her journey to Damascus, she believed, that well-chosen words could bring about a new order in the world of things. She was even able to remember a few verses in broken Arabic, which she recited to Mehdi when she needed a break from their Pinglish:

As if they cast
live coals from my heart,
offered my soul,
drank my blood!

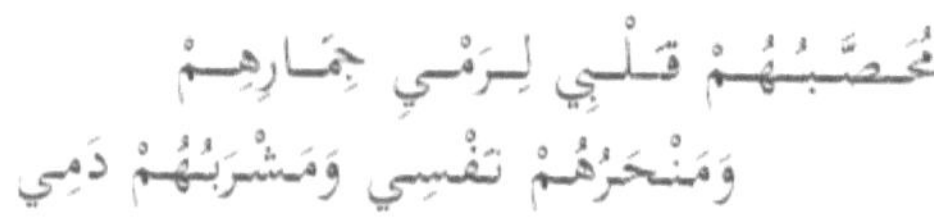

Once, as they lingered in bed on a lazy Saturday, he told her that he did not believe in God.

"That's impossible," she joked, "Your name means savior. You are the Messiah. You are the savior of humanity. How can you grow up in the Islamic Republic of Iran without believing in God?"

It was supposed to be a joke, but it fell flat. As if she were actually serious. He pressed the tips of his fingers against her nose. She stopped speaking. He smiled weakly, trying to make light of her clumsiness, and shook his head sadly.

What their tongues lacked when they were apart made them complete when they were together. They traveled together to cities outside Damascus: Aleppo, Homs, and Maʿarat al-Nuʿman, home of the eleventh century poet Abu al-ʿAlaʾ al-Maʿarri. Every time they traveled together, they faced endless strings of questions about their origins, their destinations, and their reasons for traveling together. Were they married? Were they lovers? Were they simply friends? Inquiring minds everywhere wanted to know. The best they could do was respond with polite stock answers, and curious, bewildered smiles. Instead of answering directly, they diverted the questions, turning them into conversations about language.

"I am from Iran," Mehdi would answer such questions in flawless Arabic. *Ana min Iran.* His Arabic sounded native to her ear. She was awed by his fluency in a foreign tongue.

"My companion is American." "Our countries are enemies, but we are friends," he would invariably add, anticipating the driver's reaction, and further recycling his repertoire of stock responses.

"You should set up a travel agency together," one taxi driver said good-humoredly.

"You can teach the United Nations a lot," said another.

"Maybe you can show our leaders how to rule the world," said a third.

"Together, you too can stop World War III," said a fourth.

Every one of these taxi drivers laughed at them. She didn't see what was so funny.

Five months passed. Spring was approaching, and their love was in bloom. Meanwhile, the streets were filled with signs of discontent. On 15 March, protesters marched through Damascus and Aleppo, demanding that political prisoners be released. She stopped going out for food alone. Mehdi accompanied her everywhere.

The more they traveled around Syria, the more the taxi drivers seemed filled with anxiety. She tried to get the drivers to reflect on the political situation.

"Would there be war?" she asked. She never received a straight answer.

Sometimes, Mehdi translated for her, hoping to encourage more conversation about politics. No one would speak openly.

"These walls have ears," one driver said, looking nervously at the rear-view mirror.

They celebrated the beginning of Spring, which was also Nowruz, the Persian New Year, in Aleppo, reading Persian poetry by candlelight. Three months earlier, in faraway Tunisia, a young street vendor had immolated himself, protesting the abuse he faced from the police, which he connected to the oppression of his people. Hundreds of miles away, a revolution was underway in Cairo. The tyrant Hosni Mubarak was finally deposed, and a popular new leader was installed in his place. Mohamed Morsi, with a PhD from USC. The Arab world was in revolt, and democracy was on the horizon.

Teresa brought these events up with her Arabic teacher several times during their lessons. She felt the pressure of history: a new world was being born, and she wanted to gauge whether he felt the same. He was a kind elderly man with thick glasses, and exceedingly cautious in discussing political matters.

Only when she mentioned her conversations with Mehdi, who believed that revolution was the only option, even if it had to take place through violence, did he listen in earnest. The pupils of his eyes widened in fear. Unlike Mehdi, he was convinced that Syria would remain an exception to the succession of violent overthrows that was sweeping through the Arab world.

"Who needs revolution?" he finally said when she ceased speaking. "We Syrians prefer peace. Yes, our regime is oppressive, but at least we have economic security. We know where our bread is coming from, and where it will come from tomorrow. Why give up our security for the sake of a fiction about freedom?"

As she listened to him speak, Teresa grew embarrassed by the thought that she may have divulged confidential information about her lover, and their developing intimacy. After all, he was of Shi'a origin, and they were in a Sunni country. Would Mehdi be angry, she wondered, if he had heard this conversation?

Her Arabic teacher was not concerned with her intimate revelations. He was preoccupied with the political changes on the horizon. All he could do was pray for peace.

"There will be no revolution," he concluded simply. "Syrians have too much to lose from war." After a pause he added. "I believe in God."

That was the last time she ever spoke to her teacher.

Weeks passed. By April, life in Syria had changed forever. Whereas taxi drivers had stopped talking politics, now there were completely silent, and mostly not to be found. While many students passed their days protesting on the streets as classes began to be cancelled, others retreated further into their homes, fearful of going out alone.

Damascus' streets used to be serene on Friday afternoons, but now they were filled with protestors, university students, unhappy with the regime, and unafraid to make their discontent public. Graffiti covered the walls leading all the way from the metro station to the university campus. The students held up placards in front of Damascus University, saying "*Suqut an-nizam* [down with the regime]." The radio blared more loudly than before. Evening prayers were increasingly interrupted by shouting from the streets.

Her mother sent her a message by email, a medium she rarely used. "ARE YOU OK?" she asked in the subject line. Rather than answer the question, Teresa decided it was time to leave. Escape from home by living in a war zone was no solution. Her Syrian interlude was reaching an end. Time to move on.

Damascus was changing, and Mehdi too was undergoing a transformation. One day, as she awoke alone in his apartment—he had gone to fresh bread and fruit for their breakfast—she happened to see his CV on the edge of his desk. She had never seen it before and could not resist the temptation to skim. She got out of bed, crept over to the table, and peered furtively at the white paper.

The biography given in that document did not match the story he had told her about himself at the fair the previous year. He had told her that he attended Sharif,

Iran's top university. Yet he declared himself in his CV as a graduate of Shiraz University. Mona had told her that his thesis was on Iraqi poet Badr al-Shakir al-Sayyab. Yet, he listed the PhD on his CV was listed as "complete." And the subject was not poetry at all. Rather, he was proposing a proof, using the principles of thermonuclear energy, of the certain return of the Imam.

Mehdi returned from shopping, his arms overloaded with fresh food for their breakfast. She smiled and said nothing. She feared that confronting him would lead to disaster. Besides, she reasoned, what's wrong with a little ambiguity? Surely there was a rational explanation for the discrepancies in his CV. Surely she had made an honest mistake, and when she discovered what it was, he would be exonerated entirely. Then, she remembered the hands that disturbed her the first time she saw him. She remembered how they made her think of the ruling elite, who don't know the meaning of honest work, and who maintain their grip on power by lying.

She suppressed the thought again. She preferred to believe his lies than to consider him a liar. But the more discrepancies she discovered between the stories he told her about himself and the stories she read in the documents he carried with him, the harder it became to maintain the illusion of his honesty. Nonetheless, she continued keeping quiet about her concerns. She would have to leave Syria soon anyway, so what would be the point of such a difficult conversation?

Meanwhile, anger simmered within. Her affection for Mehdi came to be mixed with contempt. He began to appear to her like a con artist, a master at using language to serve his private fantasies and his narcissistic cravings.

She had been impressed by his ability to weave between different idioms like different clothes, but now she was beginning to perceive his linguistic brilliance in a different light. She began to recognize that much of what he told her about himself, including the things that had most appealed to her, could not have been true.

In the moments when he left her alone and she had the chance to examine his desk, she found papers—documents folded over on themselves as if to conceal something—signed with different names, names he had never used for himself. In one document, he claimed membership in the IRGC, the Iranian Revolutionary Guards whom he had claimed to despise. His qualifications, his life plans, and even his identity were coming to seem suspect. His linguistic gifts began to seem to her like just another facet of his deceptions.

The more she learned about Mehdi's falsehoods, the more complicit she felt in these deceptions. The language that they had created together had enabled her to become whomever she wanted to be and to do whatever she wanted to do within the space of their shared fantasy, so long as she disregarded the truth.

Panglish had constructed for her a palace where the imagination was king, and poetry dominated everything. Having been born as an escape route, their secret language was now a trap, placing her in danger's way. Syria was rapidly hurling towards war and her affair with Mehdi was a toxic, disastrous lie.

Should I confront him? she wondered. *What if he punishes me for my discovery? This might be dangerous.* She decided it was better to keep silent. She would escape before he found out that she knew he was a fraud.

She began to wonder whether he could distinguish between fiction and reality. Then she remembered the first time she met him. *His hands.* That magical day at the book fair. And for the first time since they had met, she remembered the job offer he had told her about. She was skeptical at the time and she believed him even less now. After he had told her that he would be moving to the United States to work as a lobbyist, they had never discussed her plans again. She assumed that the offer had been retracted, or maybe she had simply misunderstood his word. After all, it was in the days before their Panglish had been fully formed, before they had understood each other perfectly. Now she knew: he had been lying to her from the beginning.

Weeks passed. Talking heads around the world oscillated between prophesying Syria's doom and promising the country's final liberation from tyranny. The one thing such predictions shared in common is that they were uttered by people with no direct contact to the country of which they spoke with such assurance.

As she prepared to leave the country, Mehdi's self-deception became increasingly absurd. Months into their language games, he told her that the job offer he had received from the US was really an email from a staff member expressing interest in working with him as a voluntary consultant. In fact, his correspondent had no idea that he wished to migrate to the United States.

"Since that plan collapsed, perhaps you can help me migrate?" Mehdi suggested one night after a particularly intense session of making love. After Teresa did not respond, he added as if to encourage her: "My English is getting better every day."

Eventually, she could not deny it anymore: his lies belonged to a long pattern of misrepresentation and exaggerations, of falsely passing himself off as someone he was not. Then she understood: her outsized vision of him, her easy belief all of his improbable claims, was the dark side of the miracle they created together when they spoke in multiple tongues. The language of their intimacy was also the language of their deception. He had insinuated himself, on false premises, into her life.

On the last day in March, on the six-month anniversary of their first meeting, Mehdi proposed another overnight trip to Aleppo.

"Don't worry," he said. "It's safe. I'll take care of you."

She laughed, cringing within. By this point in their relationship, she was afraid to refuse.

As they waited together in the elevator that would take them to their hotel room near the Aleppo citadel, the operator initiated a conversation with Mehdi in Arabic. The operator was so impressed by Mehdi's fluent Arabic that he suggested that he write a novel in Arabic. Instead of being flattered, Mehdi was taken aback. Teresa could tell by the offended expression on his face. She was surprised when she learned why.

"That won't happen," Mehdi responded, "I'm a *critic*, not a novelist. I judge the world of literature. I don't produce fictions."

"You'd make a better novelist than you realize," Teresa told him, when they got off the elevator.

She trusted that he wouldn't catch what she really meant as the truth hammered in her head: *you could write fiction because you're a compulsive liar. You lie more than you like to tell the truth. When Mona told me you were brilliant, she forgot to add: a brilliant liar.* She kept her mouth shut, not wishing to instigate an argument during their final days together.

Alongside her fear of Mehdi, her contempt for herself in these final days grew.

They spent their last night together pouring over dictionaries, making up new phrases in Panglish. "I am the night that shines in the black hole of your stomach," he said proudly, with complete disregard for the proper order of speech.

"*Man in chashmeh-yi hastam, ke to mikhondi pish az khubidi* (I am the eye that you read before going to sleep)," she replied, with an equal disregard for logic, sense, and meaning.

He asked her if she remembered any verses by Ibn Arabi that she could recite to him. She paused a long time over the lines, trying to imagine them rustling around in his mind. Then, as if suddenly possessed by demons—otherwise how could she have managed to speak Arabic so perfectly?—she recited:

Yearning sought the highlands,
consolation the plain
and here I'm stranded
between Najd and Tiham.

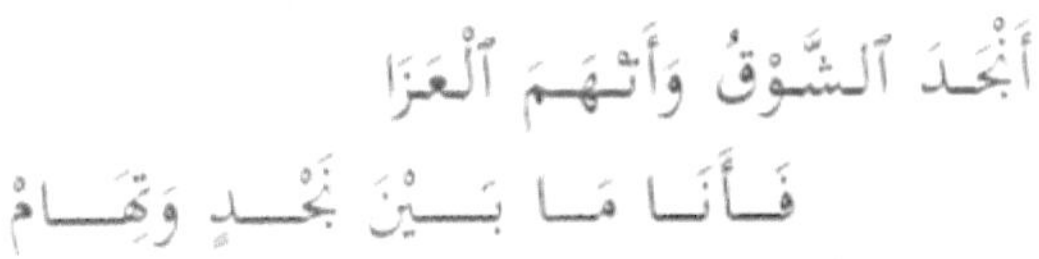

He stared at her in surprise. She had never been able to speak Arabic like that. What had happened? He continued with the poem:

> *Opposites never*
> *to be joined—*
> *Undone, unstrung*
> *Harmony*

وَهُمَا ضِــدَّانِ لَــنْ يَجْتَمِعَا

فَشَــتَّانِ مَــا لَــهُ ٱلـدَّهْـرَ نِـظَـامْ

She couldn't recall the next lines, but she did remember the end. She recited:

> *I live on and*
> *in living die*
> *Farewell to her, then,*
> *and to patience, farewell.*

مَا حَيَاتِي بَعْدَهُمْ إِلَّا ٱلْفَنَا

فَعَلَيْهَا وَعَلَى ٱلـصَّـبْرِ ٱلسَّـلَامْ

After months of speaking his tongue, it seemed appropriate that they were saying goodbye in a language that was foreign to them both.

She wanted to find a resting place for their words, a perpetuity that would last long after they had parted.

Where they would hang suspended between the world of the imagination and the world they were forced to inhabit, a world now on the brink of war.

She had to end the relationship, and leave Syria. It would be easier to do that if she didn't have to say goodbye to him.

She recited Ibn Arabi to him again, as they lay in bed, her head resting on his chest, his fingers stroking her hair. He repeated the same verses back.

Of course, she didn't tell him it was the end. What would have been the point of that?

That night, before she drifted into a fragmented, intermittent sleep, she imagined what she might have said to him if she could have trusted him. She would have told him that his miraculous ability to speak in tongues did not give him the right to fabricate his way through life, to lie to her, and to falsify himself. *If you had not tried so hard to impress me, so hard that it led you to lie to me, maybe— just maybe—we could have built a life together*, she thought to herself. *Working wonders with language does not give you the right to lie, especially not to the woman you claimed to love.*

She did not say any of this to him. War was looming on the horizon in Damascus. She had to leave. Their love was fragile, trembling with disaster on the horizon, just like the country where it had been conceived. She had already booked her flight without telling him, and was due to fly tomorrow afternoon to Istanbul, and then onwards to Chicago, where she would take the Amtrak to Urbana. Her parents still kept a room for her in their home.

Her mother would, she hoped, be happy to see her for once, happy to have her daughter out of harm's way. It would be a bittersweet homecoming, a kind of defeat, but it was surely better than continuing to inhabit a war zone, locked into a doomed relationship with a fraudulent lover.

Her sleep more like a reverie, during which her mind wandered through the fantasy world that had been constructed of their brief lives together. Wrinkles in the fabric of time. In that beautiful foreign land of their love, the waterways and aqueducts were all made of Panglish. Streets could only be crossed on gondolas. No one lacked a lover because love was everywhere. Everyone was a stranger to each other, yet they were also in love.

She remembered the café in Sarouja where she first was melted by his turquoise irises, the book fair where he has taught her how to bargain and supplied her with books she would treasure for the rest of her life. The same place where he had first used language with her to lie. He had a gift for reciting poems in multiple tongues. Her mind's eye pictured the bridges they had built from their words, binding East and West, Iran and the US, via Syria, Persian, and English, in a passionate embrace. It was a sweet dream, which would soon be shattered by a violent dawn.

3.

Nafs

What they next said, what they said instead, they forgot:
there are questions which, if not asked at the start,
are not asked later, so those they never did ask.
—Elizabeth Bowen, *The Heat of the Day*

When she was awarded a year-long fellowship in Budapest, Teresa Wallace was given the opportunity to invite anyone she wanted, anywhere in the world, to visit her during her stay in Hungary. She invited a famous scholar whose book she adored, and he declined. And then she remembered Yasin, the Uzbek scholar with whom she had crossed paths a decade earlier, in Amman. True, he might have no interest in Budapest, but what was the harm in asking? They shared a passion for manuscripts.

She searched her apartment for his number, and came across a piece of scrap paper on which he had scribbled his name and phone number years ago. There was no email address. She crossed her fingers and dialed his number in Tashkent. Someone answered in heavily accented Russian: "*Allo?*" She could tell immediately that the speaker was not a native speaker of the language.

She explained who she was and why she was calling. She asked if he remembered her. He said he had never forgotten her.

He was delighted by the invitation to visit her in Budapest. The visa process was set in motion by the institute, which also arranged for his lecture. Meanwhile, Teresa waited, unsure of what the visit would bring. She was open to anything, so long as it meant change.

She finished lecturing to a nearly empty classroom at the University of Iowa. The class was called "Comparative Democracies," but she had veered far from the subject matter, ranging over topics such as Mongolian horses to medieval poetry. Most students had stopped attending. She wondered if a large number of student complaints might lead to losing her job, and then she realized that she didn't care. She was ready to abandon academia.

Yet there was a small contingent of students who attended every lecture religiously, regardless of how far she veered off topic. She was coming to realize through these lectures that she'd made a mistake when she went into political science. She should have chosen a field closer to the soul, something that enabled her to create, like painting or bookmaking. She was grateful for the handful of political science majors who welcomed the break from lectures on supply-side economics, international relations, and post-Cold War security. This contingent of true believers erupted in cheers when she announced the end of the course. The semester was over. Life was about to take a new turn.

The next morning, Teresa boarded the shuttle bus to the Iowa City Municipal Airport, from where she would fly to Chicago, and from there directly to Budapest. As the bus raced past cornfields and silos overflowing with grain, she reflected that this might be her last chance to enjoy this godforsaken, gold-tinged, vexing landscape that she both despised and loved. She had read Willa Cather with a passion since childhood, and loved her rhapsodies of the

American Midwest. Why could she not follow Cather's example and learn to love this barren terrain?

The flight was long and uneventful, aside from her violent mental cogitations. She passed the night in the sky reading Gershom Scholem's account of his friendship with Walter Benjamin. Reading of Scholem's efforts to make Benjamin reject Marxism and embrace his Jewish origins reminded Teresa of her own friendships, as well as her many failed love affairs. She wondered why she seemed most comfortable among strangers, and so ill at ease among her intimate relations. *Where does the boundary between self and other begin? When do we stop lying to others and start becoming ourselves?*

She arrived three days before Yasin was due to arrive. She passed these empty days in pleasant solitude, exploring the town in anticipation of his arrival, creating spaces for her new temporary home, Budapest, before it would be shaped by him. *What would it be like to meet him after a decade*, she wondered. *Has he changed? Will he think that I have? He'll see everything about me that I've concealed from myself.*

In the intervening decade, he'd received fellowships, major research foundations in Germany, Austria, and France. She'd secured an academic position, albeit in a place overrun with cornfields and cows which she perpetually dreamed of leaving. She was becoming permanently displaced. The world was turning against her, and against people like her. Fascism loomed on the horizon, and particularly in Hungary, where Jobbik, the party of the current President Viktor Orbán, had just witnessed a resounding victory. Refugees were being turned back at the border. Jews, Roma, and Muslims were coming under attack.

Every day since her arrival, she crossed the Chain Bridge that stretched over the Danube. Built by two Englishmen in 1849, the bridge symbolized the unification of the two sides of the city: Buda and Pest. Often, she crossed twice, as the sun rose and as the sun set. On one side of the bridge was the apartment where she was staying on Raoul Wallenberg Street, on the Pest side of the bridge. On the Buda side, opposite the banks of the Danube, was the main campus of Central European University. This was its last year in Budapest. Beginning in September, it would relocate to Vienna, and all the students and faculty would have to move to Austria.

Teresa suppressed her fears about the future of Hungary, of Europe, and of the world and compelled herself to prepare for Yasin's arrival on Friday. They were both, as far as she could tell, childless, and immersed in scholarship. She was ready for something new, in life as well as work and eagerly awaited the inspiration his visit would bring.

She began waiting for his call at 7AM on Friday morning. She had emailed him several days earlier, asking him to call as soon as he arrived, but the phone stayed stubbornly silent on its handset. She stared at the black handle, wondering when it would emit a sound. Finally, after fifty-four minutes and thirty-two seconds of waiting (she had been keeping time on her stopwatch), there was a ring.

"Hello?" she said. "*Allo*," a voice replied. It was Yasin, addressing her in the same accented Russian that revealed his Uzbek background.

They exchanged a few pleasantries, until their conversation came to a standstill. She had not spoken Russian in years. The words did not flow as easily as they had in Amman. She broke the silence by suggesting that they see each other face to face. After all, he was only two floors beneath her.

"*Mozhno*?" she said simply, leaving her meaning open to interpretation. She translated back to herself: *may I?*

"*Mozhno*," he replied with equal brevity, turning her question into an answer. She hung up and made preparations to descend.

When she saw him standing at the threshold of his door, she realized that she would have recognized him anywhere, in the streets of Budapest or the cornfields of Iowa. He was darker in complexion than before and his hair was scruffier than she remembered from a decade ago. He had grown a beard. But he was the same unassuming Yasin with thick glasses and a boyish smile on his face. Yasin explained that he had not been able to sleep on the flight from Tashkent and had been catching up on lost sleep since he arrived. That was why he was late in calling her. But now he was refreshed and ready to see the town.

"Shall we explore the city?" he proposed. "I've always wanted to see the Danube."

It was around seven in the evening. The sun lingered on the horizon, its ochre seeping a bloody haze over the Danube. Their first stop was the Chain Bridge, at each end of which stood two majestic grey lions, each made of greyish stone. In the dusk, the bridge appeared to be suspended in the water. When they reached the bridge's end, on the Pest side of Budapest, they meandered down 6

October Street. The name of the street captured Yasin's attention. Although it sounded Soviet, he could not place the date. Teresa explained that it referred to an anti-Soviet rebellion. On 6 October 1956, the anti-Soviet communist László Rajk was publicly buried in a memorial to the victims of the Stalin-backed purges from several years prior. 6 October was a prelude to 23 October 1956, the date of the Hungarian Revolution.

Teresa recited these details with enthusiasm, while Yasin grew weary of the flow of information. His Soviet education had made him skeptical of history. He turned to her with a smile and took her hand in his.

"Shall we have pizza?" he suggested, as if it were an exotic food. "There is no good pizza in Uzbekistan."

They crossed the bridge again, to the Buda side of city. They ascended the winding staircase of an Italian restaurant at the end of an arcade that seemed to date back centuries. He ordered a pizza with salmon and feta cheese. She ordered a pizza with arugula, mozzarella, and broccoli.

He asked her about life in Iowa. Was it like the rest of America? he wanted to know. He had only been to the U.S. once, San Francisco in the 1990s.

"America is many countries," she began. "The South is a bastion of bigotry. The North is a land of elite education and heavy snowfall. The American West is a land of adobe houses and deserts. As for the Midwest, where I was born, it is also a country unto itself, of prairies that stretch across the horizon, cornfields, and many white people. Too many white people. I'm sick of white people," she said with a self-deprecating smile.

She guessed that she must have sounded like she was talking nonsense to Yasin. At the same time, she could not deny that she enjoyed lecturing to him about the country she used to think of as her home, and which she could now only regard as a parody of its former self. To distance herself from it while asserting her authority over it. She was becoming a true expatriate, someone who could say hello and goodbye to her homeland at will.

Yasin asked whether she liked living in the Midwest.

"No," she said. "In Iowa I feel like an alien in my own country. And I fear it's getting worse. People are becoming more nationalist, more prejudiced, more racist. Also, it's far from where my family lives now."

"Family," Yasin repeated the last word, as if he failed to recognize its meaning.

"Yes, family," she repeated.

He stared deep into her eyes. "Who is your family?"

"Me, my sisters, and my mother."

"No husband?"

"No, no husband."

From her fieldwork in Central Asia, Teresa had come to expect the husband question. Equally familiar was the question that followed: when would she start having children? In most places where she conducted research, it was the first question on her interlocutors' tongue. Generally, the inquiry aimed to ascertain whether she conformed to a woman her age, reaching the end of her childbearing years. She was thirty-five. Everyone expected her to be preparing for children—preferably a boy *and* a girl, but just a boy was enough—and a husband. A career was optional. As an elderly woman in the Uzbek village where she conducted fieldwork had told her in a spirit of sisterly camaraderie: a woman needs only two things: a husband and a son. Anything else, she added, is a luxury.

When Yasin, his eyebrows gently arched, posed to her the husband question his curiosity seemed somehow more personal and less a cultural reflex. Whereas normally she greeted questions about her personal life with polite silence, with Yasin, she was moved to speak openly. She railed against the sexism that scrutinized her private life whenever she was in the field, and lamented that a woman was assumed to be incomplete without a man. Yasin laughed lightly and flashed a look that to her implied a deeper understanding than could be communicated in words.

When they finished eating, they crossed the bridge again and wandered down Andrássy Avenue, Budapest's main commercial thoroughfare. Yasin pulled out a pack of cigarettes and began to smoke. The smell affected her strangely, as though someone were rubbing the palm of her hand. They passed fountains, glass windows, row after row of stores with greetings in multiple scripts pasted on their doors. They walked around the Ferris wheel at Erzsebet Square, until finally they were surrounded by benches and trees. It was late at night and the park was deserted. Pairs of lovers were seated on the benches, lost in each other's arms beneath flickering lamps.

"Let's sit down," he suggested.

He took her hand in his, as he had done earlier that day when they crossed the bridge. She expected his hand to move away from hers once they were seated, but it remained pressed on her palm. His soft, respectful, but nonetheless firm grip called to mind a nurse measuring her patient's heartbeat. Teresa recalled Yasin's question about her family, and she wondered again why he was so curious.

It was the first and last time he ever inquired about her personal circumstances.

His hand remained steadily on hers, as if it were natural for a man and a woman who had spent only a few hours together to hold hands. As if her hand belonged to him and his hand belonged to her.

When they arrived back at the apartments on Raoul Wallenberg street, he invited her inside.

"I want to show you the files of a manuscript that I found in the library of Oriental Studies," he explained, "plus I'd love to make you a warm cup of the tea I brought you from Tashkent."

It was an offer she could not refuse.

As soon as they entered, he set the kettle on for tea. The Institute had set him up in a luxurious two-story apartment with two large bedrooms and two full bathrooms. It was a step above her more spartan accommodations.

He opened his laptop and began searching through files. They passed the next three hours seated like that, with his head bent over his computer while sifting through the digital files he had accumulated from his many years of working in the archives. Meanwhile, gigabytes of manuscript data migrated onto the external drive he had brought to share with her.

As they sat hunched over his computer, Yasin's hand stayed firmly fixed on her lap. Teresa arrested its movement, but she was pleased. She wanted to touch him back in the way he was touching her, but she also did not want to do anything that she might later regret. She had been celibate for over three years.

If we have sex, it might be my last time for many years to come, she reflected, *perhaps for the remainder of my life.*

There was no need to be so fatalistic, she realized, but the day they had spent together seemed so perfect, so fragile and unrepeatable. She wanted to make the memory permanent, and that seemed to require a special kind of intimacy. She wanted to delay their intimacy as long as possible, so that, when the time came for their bodies to join, it would be etched all the more powerfully in her memory.

So, while she enjoyed the tentative contact he made with her body, she blocked his hand from moving beyond her lap. When Yasin's fingers began to wander, crawling over her knees and up her legs, Teresa stood up.

"It's time for me to go to bed," she said.

"Why don't you stay longer? I'd like to make you another cup of Uzbek tea."

She said she needed to go to sleep. In reality, it was not sleepiness but a desire to create a space in her memory for what was to come, that led her back to her room.

Teresa spent the rest of the night thinking about Yasin from the privacy of her bed. She wondered what it would be like to return to her bed in the aftermath of having slept with him. How would she feel when he was gone? Would she experience the same old lingering loneliness lying in bed alone? Would the banks of the Danube look the same in the aftermath of their union as it did before they made love?

She called him as soon as she awoke. The sun's rays were filling the Danube with light. He suggested another walk across the bridge. These walks were becoming a daily ritual. They reached the same park, just beyond the Ferris wheel, where they had lingered together the day before and sat down on a bench facing the tallest fountain.

Although the water had stopped flowing, children continued to play. They began talking about the manuscripts he had discovered in the Oriental Library.

"Maybe you should quit your job and come to work with me in Tashkent?" he asked.

She froze with excitement. Was that a marriage proposal? Then she glanced at him and could see that he was joking.

"Of course," he added, "no one with a job like yours would ever leave it."

He took her hand in his as he had done before. This time, however, his hand moved, from her lap to her cheek, to her lips. While his fingers rested on her lips, the moment she had been anticipating the night before had arrived. She closed her eyes. Their lips touched.

The kiss was polite, restrained, and gentle. When he whispered into her ear, "Let's go home," his passion kindled into something else. His shyness became desire, a desire that briefly overwhelmed her world.

"This is nafs," he said.

"What?" she asked. She didn't understand.

"It has many translations. Psyche. Ego. Breathe. In Sufism, nafs means to be dominated by your animal side. I'll explain later."

Given that his visit has passed in discussions of forgotten manuscripts, she was surprised by his way of making love, which was strangely violent and hard to reconcile with traditional Islamic values. He undressed her and immediately began performing oral sex on her, with his penis pointed directly above her mouth. Then he slipped on a condom with a speed that suggested someone who had done it many times. To think that she had taken him for a virgin! Had he brought condoms in the expectation that they would have sex? Or did he carry them with him everywhere he went?

When they were done, they rested in each other's arms. Eyes wide open, they peered into the dark, black night. He lit one of the cigarettes he had purchased on Andrássy Avenue the night before. Behind him, on the other side of the bed, a pile of condoms were heaped into a crumbling pyramid.

As if from habit, she imagined becoming his wife. *I'm not fit to be a wife to anyone*, she thought to herself. She was not suited to look after a husband or bow to her partner's needs. Independence and freedom were the foundation of her existence. A long-distance relationship might suit her better, she decided.

As she always did after sex, her brain processed what she would do if she were pregnant. And then she remembered: three years earlier, she had been sterilized. She had not had sex since and had nearly forgotten that she no longer had the capacity to bear children. The procedure's name—Essure—was symbolically significant. Its phonemic proximity to 'erasure' mirrored its function. Essure had erased her biological potential for motherhood. Her body still remembered the abortion she had in Amman, just before she met Yasin. Ten years later, it still scarred her memory. That experience led her to decide that sterilisation was necessary, regardless of the cost, regardless of her many years of abstinence. After her sterilisation, she was finally at peace. At long last, she could be certain she would never bring a child into the world.

My tubes are tied, metaphorically and literally, she thought while lying in bed. Yasin was propped up on a nearby pillow, silently smoking a cigarette. *I will never bear a child.*

In addition to relieving her of the burden of fertility, Essure made the pregnancy prevention function of condoms redundant. The only reason to use a condom now was to guard against disease. But Yasin was Muslim, Teresa reasoned. Furthermore, he was shy, polite, and short, the absolute antithesis of the alpha male. Surely sex was a rare occurrence in his life? She decided to mention her sterilisation operation.

"I can't get pregnant." she began. "I had an operation."

"An operation? For what?"

"Not to have kids."

Her statement was followed by silence. Then he repeated after her, just as he had slowly repeated the word "family" the night earlier, in a tone that registered her words while ignoring their meaning, "Not to have kids."

His repetitions always seemed to contain new questions. She elaborated, "I believe in adoption. What about you? Do you want kids?"

Another lengthy silence. At last, he said, "Kids? I already have them."

Teresa froze. At first his answer made no sense. How could he have kids without having a wife? Was his wife dead? Was he divorced? A few minutes of these reflections passed, until, finally, she understood.

"You're married," she said.

He did not respond.

"And your wife?" she asked as her intonation rose, "how old is she?" She did not want to know the answer, but it was the only sane and civil question she could think of to ask.

"Thirty-three," he said mildly.

"Does she work?"

"No."

"Do you pity her?" It was the only thing she could think of to say. The question she wanted to ask most, whether he loved his wife, frightened her. She could not summon the words to her lips. Either way, the outcome would bring sorrow. If he didn't love his wife, that would be tragic. If he loved his wife, what was he doing in bed with her in Budapest?

Finally, after a long pause, Yasin answered, "Yes."

That was it. There was nothing more to say or do, other than to absorb the shock of his silent lie. They had connected profoundly without knowing even the most basic details of each other's lives. It was her first extramarital affair, the first time she had made love to a married man, and she hadn't even known that he was married when it happened.

They stumbled out of bed. He hurried to put a shirt on. "Are you Muslim?" she asked.

"Yes," he said.

"Then how do you explain this?" She pointed to his uncovered and still slightly erect penis, which he quickly concealed beneath a sheet. "Was that an Islamic act?" she asked sarcastically.

"Even believers do wrong," he said. "I told you earlier about nafs, remember? Our lust makes us commit evil acts."

"So you think what we just did is wrong?" she asked. "I think rather that what we did was right, and that your lying is what was wrong."

He had no response. She waited and realized he had nothing to say. She decided to launch into a short diatribe, to lecture in a way she always did when there was nothing to be done: "Marriage is the world's biggest source of inequality. And the greatest generator of suffering."

Her mind swept over her past life: as a daughter growing up in a household dominated by a violent father, and as a wife, married to an abusive husband. These chapters in her life that she wanted to forget were returning in full force now.

Finally, she stumbled on an accusation that she knew would hit home, striking him with some of the pain he had inflicted on her: "I hate your lying hypocrisy."

Yasin stared at her silently, as if unable to fathom her meaning. If he had been offended by her accusation, his face did not show it. Perhaps, she reflected, this was the first time he had had heard such sentiments.

Finally, she asked, "How would you like it if your wife did with another man what you just did with me?"

"I'd be furious," he said without missing a beat, as if the very possibility of his wife's infidelity was an insult to his manhood.

"You see?" Teresa smiled, although she was angry. "That's what I mean. That's what I call hypocrisy. This is patriarchy. Simply put, it means that you apply to men standards different from the ones you apply to women. It's much worse than nafs."

He edged away from her and reached for another cigarette. Then he went to the window ledge and lit the stub. His face was placid, as serene as the Danube on a winter night. He was withdrawing from their intimacy. He feared her rage but did not cherish her affection. They watched each other without moving, their figures illumined only by the moonlight outside. It was pitch black within.

After sitting motionless for several minutes, Teresa moved to the ledge where Yasin was sitting. She wanted to sit next to him. The scent of his cigarettes filled her with the desire to be touched. She wanted to make love. She had forgotten her anger from a moment earlier, and the hypocrisy that had recently repelled her now seemed like less a mark of moral failure than the kind of contradiction in which everyone is implicated.

Why had she not guessed that he was married? Why had she not asked? It was the hypocrisy of marriage rather than his deception that moved her to rage. Why couldn't he sleep with whomever he wanted to, just as she could?

Her fingers grazed his unshaven cheeks. He turned to the side. She wanted to scream at him for lying to her, for concealing the most intimate details of his personal life. At the same time, and just as powerfully, she wanted to embrace him. When would she have the opportunity to do this again, especially with someone who shared her passion of manuscripts?

He backed away. She realized with a shock that he wanted to erase the memories they had just created together.

"Can we go for a walk?" he suggested and gestured towards the window. The moon had vanished from view and an artificial light, hoisted over the middle of the bridge, shimmered over the Danube. Its ripples reminded her of his hands.

"Not tonight," she said coldly. "I have to go to bed."

He nodded, his eyes averted from her gaze. "Sleep well," he said gently.

The next day passed uneventfully. She caught up with sleep and worked on an overdue article, while he prepared his lecture for Monday. Around five in the afternoon, he called her. They agreed to meet by the stone lion at the entrance to the bridge.

Once they saw each other, the tension that had simmered all day dissipated. They crossed back and forth along the many bridges that bisected the Danube as the river winds through the city, dividing and uniting Buda and Pest. This time, they did not hold hands. A space intervened between them, like an electronic fence that sent shock waves through anyone who dared to trespass.

"Are you Muslim?" She asked again, fascinated by the ability of men to profess fidelity to a faith they did not observe in their personal lives. "I mean, are you a believer?"

When he said yes, she asked how it was possible for a married man who regarded himself as Muslim to sleep with other women.

"I already explained," he said. "Nafs. Not all Muslims act as their faith commands. Like you, we sometimes follow our passions."

She felt a twitch of pain. She'd done her research the night before, learned that nafs was associated with spiritual degradation. It was a kind of selfishness. She also learned something that she suspected Yasin did not know: the Arabic term derived from the Hebrew word *nephesh*, meaning breathe.

"I bet you didn't know that nafs is the beginning of consciousness," she said.

"No," he corrected her. "Nafs refers to the lower faculty, the passions."

"So, when you made love to me, it was with your nafs and not your heart?"

He nodded vaguely. The question made him uncomfortable. His shyness, which she remembered from the conference in Amman where they met, returned. Then he added softly, "I'm not sure I understand your question."

"Unlike you, I made love with my heart, not with my nafs," she said. "I respect Islam, but I am against your religion. Sex is not evil. It is the breath of life. That is my nafs."

He remained silent for several minutes.

Finally, he said: "Are you hungry?"

The had reached the end of the bridge. The Danube glistened in the silvery rays of the setting sun. Clouds blotted the sky like cotton. An orange striped lifeboat bobbed up and down on the gentle waves. Minutes passed as his question lingered in the air. She was tired of talking. *What is the point of words when we only use them to lie to each other?*

"I'm hungry. Shall we have pizza again?"

After she said goodbye to Yasin that night, and they went to their separate apartments, she decided to quit her job at the University of Iowa and become a bookbinder. She wanted to make love for a profession, not to another human body, but to books, with her hands.

4.

When You Are Old

Teresa didn't want to go. She had too much to worry about, too many distractions. She preferred to let her pain incubate, and to observe the festering of her wounds. So when her elderly neighbor Beatrice woke her up, shortly past midnight, to celebrate Easter and share a boiled egg, as red as blood, she was both irritated and bemused. What kind of person bangs on their neighbor's door in the middle of the night to share an egg? she wondered to herself.

Beatrice informed her that her son wanted to show her Old Tbilisi, and to introduce her to the history and culture of the city where he had been born and raised. Teresa agreed. But she was less than pleased.

"I'm leaving for America the following day," she warned her neighbor, "So we'll have to finish early."

Beatrice shook Teresa's hand before she parted that night, winked slyly, and insisted she take another egg. "I'll be gone that day," Beatrice added before she parted, "But you and Irakli will have fun."

All that month, Teresa had been cooped up in her apartment. Meditating. Mostly about a man she had never met, but whom she knew better than her own soul. They shared in common a passion for certain obscure subjects, like Arabic epigraphy and Persian palaeography. More than that, they shared expertise in the peculiar annotations that itinerate.

53

Sogdian merchants of early modern Central Asia made on Arabic manuscripts, in a handwriting devised specifically for this purpose. These merchants, whose scripts no one had ever fully deciphered, inscribed their vernaculars in cobalt blue ink, using a curvaceous undotted calligraphic style, as if to signify that their pasts could not be vanquished by the new Islamic dispensation. Scholarly attempts to relate the inscriptions to other Iranian languages, such as Yaghnobi and Ghori, had fallen flat. No one alive was able to decipher them.

Working together with the philologist, Teresa succeeded in cracking one of the most difficult scripts. But many more scripts remained to be deciphered. These mysterious scripts, which only they could understand, and only by working together slowly and intimately, caused them to fall in love. Or, more precisely, caused her to fall in love with him. If her love for him was reciprocated, he never let on. But it was impossible for her to entirely discount the possibility of his love. How else could they have worked such magic together? Every time she completed an article with him, she had her own private orgasm.

Their expert knowledge was shared by no one. From the beginning of their acquaintance, before they had even exchanged words, she knew she was destined to fall in love with a philologist, but she had not been prepared for the blast when it hit her. Their connection—forged over months of email, of electronic intimacies dense with imputed meanings never articulated—was as fleeting as it was tantalizing. It consisted of questions about words no one else knew or could understand, even if they had been told their meanings. Together, they luxuriated in the verses of Hafez and Sa'di, both of whom the Sogdian merchants cited extensively in their peculiar script. Sometimes the merchants included these quotations in their original classical Persian form. At other times, they translated the poems into their vernaculars, multiplying the Babel of tongues enshrined in the old manuscripts.

No one could understand these languages as well as he did. That was why she loved him.

Every day for almost a month, Teresa and the philologist exchanged messages. They were both enthralled by the archive they were creating. It was a time capsule for the next generation of scholars. They bonded over the marginalia that only they could decipher. Like everything else in their relationship, Teresa and the philologist shared their manuscripts

electronically, using material Teresa had scanned during an earlier research visit to the Pamirs on the Tajik side of the border (Afghanistan was in a state of war back then, in 2008). They compared variants. They speculated about which reading was more certain, and what caused the divergences, among texts, scripts, calligraphies, and visions. Together, they entered another era, time travelling as only philologists can time travel, through the many mountains these manuscripts had traversed before they landed on the internet. Teresa and the philologist lived within the materiality of Islamic texts, which became the substance of their relationship, and the foundation of their love.

And then, four months into their friendship, he dropped a bomb.

"My wife just gave birth to a baby," he wrote her in a note that was much briefer than usual. Weeks passed with no response.

The worst part was that he seemed to have no idea what it meant to her. She didn't even know he was married. When she had him entirely to herself, by email, it never occurred to her to speculate about his relations with other women.

His next message began: "Aren't you going to congratulate me?"

Congratulate him she could not do. A baby? She didn't even know he had a wife. Or was it that she didn't want to know? In fact, she had never asked. The bomb dropped by the philologist only proved one of her longest-standing convictions: brilliant men feel the need to separate their intellectual passions with their bodily hungers. Women want men who are intelligent and emotionally attentive. Men want something else. Women for them can only be one or the other. Career versus family. Passion versus intellect. Madonna versus whore. Men are in search of ego masturbation, not intellectual equality. The smarter they are, the lower they go.

Teresa did not respond to that message. Surely, he didn't need her congratulations. Instead, she lashed out by writing a scholarly article about the low status of women at the Samanid court. Yes, there were token exceptions, female queens, Scheherazades of various (usually disreputable) backgrounds, prostitutes, courtesans, harem singers. These whores and harem singers influenced male rulers in unseen ways. But the main thrust of her argument was easy to prove. Even powerful women could only exercise their power invisibly. Samanid women were not public intellectuals who held the world in the palm of their hands. Instead, their bodies were mere stepping-stones for men seeking to dominate the world.

Now that her unrealized love affair with the philologist was officially over before it had even begun, Teresa promised herself that she would make the most of her stay in Tbilisi. She wanted to start a new research agenda, and to file away the Sogdian merchant scripts in the dark recesses of her brain, in a place she would only access twenty years into the future. But forgetting was proving more difficult than she had bargained for. It was easier to lean, slowly, into the pain, and to dwell there forever. Instead of venturing out into the archives as she had planned to do when she arrived in Tbilisi, so as to crack one of the scripts she and the philologist had been working on when he dropped the bomb, Teresa found herself in bed, day after day, imagining herself reading manuscripts together with the philologist in bed, their bodies as intertwined as they flipped through the pages of a worm-eaten manuscript page, hovering over desiccated colophons, trying to decipher the Sogdian merchant script that they would then translate for the world.

Teresa didn't want to see Old Tbilisi. She agreed to accompany Irakli only because she knew it would be good for her, giving her a much needed distraction from the man she would never know in the flesh, from their virtual intimacies, from the languages they had created together, languages that still, after nearly a month of his silence, clawed deep beneath the surface of her soul.

Irakli didn't have a car. For some reason, she had been expecting that he would drive her to the top of Nariqala, Old Tbilisi's fortress. She must have misunderstood Beatrice's proposal. Instead, they walked down Rustaveli Avenue, past coffee shops and ice-cream parlours, past the

Hilton, through the arcades beneath the red roof of Tbilisi's largest theatre, named after the medieval poet, Rustaveli. It had recently been renovated and its gingerbread striped walls shined beneath the sun. Tbilisi's main thoroughfare was bustling with booksellers and businessmen. Finally, they reached the red-striped walls of the mayor's residence. It was a hot day for the middle of May. Teresa regretted that she had not brought water with her.

Irakli apologized for not speaking English. There was nothing to apologize for, Teresa insisted. English was a language she had no desire to speak. It was the language in which her love for the philologist had taken root, notwithstanding the many tongues they shared. One of the few languages she did not share with the philologist was Russian, which made it an attractive medium for starting life over again. A second language they didn't share was Georgian. Moving between Russian and Georgian with Irakli, her self-appointed guide to Old Tbilisi's monuments, became a source of consolation, distracting her from her feelings of abandonment.

They exited Rustaveli Avenue. Irakli escorted Teresa through the medieval alleyways and dark corridors that stretched all the way from Freedom Square to Nariqala, perched on top of a hill that overlooked the city. Irakli explained how, in centuries past, the carriages of the rich and the carts of the poor had maneuvered over potholes and through dim alleyways. First tsarist and then Soviet regimes had changed these streets, turning the oversized mansions into communal apartments, widening the narrow passageways, and adding plumbing. Still, much remained the same from tsarist times and even earlier.

The churches did not interest her much, but the sulphur baths of Abanotubani (Bath District) were stunning. Dating back to the seventh century, and attributed to King Irakli, these baths were refurbished in the sixteenth century by Tbilisi's Persian, Armenian, and Azeri merchants, who tried to buttress their reputations by displaying their love for their

adopted city. Now the baths were one of the most striking Persianate architectural monuments in Tbilisi's cityscape. Across the street was the ancient Metekhi Church, near which the martyr Abo of Tbilisi sacrificed his life in the eighth century for refusing to convert to Islam. Abo was the only Arab saint in the Georgian pantheon.

To the right of the sulphur baths, the Blue Bath's faux minarets hovered above. They were more stunning even than the mosques that adorned the lavishly illustrated manuscripts Teresa and the philologist had shared. The blue and gold tiles covering the Blue Bath's walls belonged to an age of peaceful exchanges between peoples of different faiths, languages, and ethnicities: Muslims, Christians, Armenians, Georgians, and Azeris. That era was long past, even if these monuments had the power to evoke nostalgia for times past.

Back in those days, when Tbilisi was still a crossroads for oriental civilizations, bathers cared only about having their bodies rubbed down in soap, of being cleansed from the impurities that had accumulated on their skin, so that they could return to the street, to selling and trading their merchandise with the other merchants of Old Tbilisi. Now, by contrast,

Irakli, her self-appointed guide, couldn't refrain from making snide remarks about the recent influx of Africans and Iranians into Tbilisi. He seemed to think that these foreigners posed a danger to the survival of the Georgian people. Every country has its flaws, Teresa reflected to herself, but how ironic that racism should flourish here, of all places, in Old Tbilisi, a city that had for so long been idealized as a place of tolerance, not least by Irakli himself.

Following closely behind Irakli, Teresa climbed the steps to Nariqala. The old fort was mostly in ruins now. Messages were scrawled on its walls in many different alphabets. Like so much of Tbilisi's past, although originally built by Georgians, who optimistically called it Shuristsikhe ("undefeatable fort"), Nariqala was soon taken over by the Umayyads, and then by the Mongols, who renamed it Narinqala ("little fort"), perhaps hoping to convey their majestic power through the diminutive. When the Mongols left Georgia in the thirteenth century, the n intervening between nari and qala was removed. So it remained: Nariqala, one of many words that entered the Georgian language from the east, with few contemporary Georgians conscious of its original meaning.

Teresa was exhausted by the time they had ascended half the stairs. She concealed her exhaustion by gulping down air. She yearned to go home. She wanted to lean into the pain of the philologist's revelation and his ensuing silence. How could she bear to look at another manuscript in the Sogdian script? How could she continue with her work, now that the

philologist was gone from her life, now that his affiliation with another woman and his baby was public knowledge? Now that she could no longer mistake their virtual intimacies for something more? As she was immersed in thinking of the merchants' script that she had deciphered together with the philologist, Teresa stumbled on a gold-plated tile that resembled the ones that covered the Blue Bath's facade. Irakli watched silently as she bent down to pick it up.

"Keep it," he advised. "It will bring you good luck."

Teresa smiled. She stroked the tile with her fingers, turned it on its side. Irakli's advice was worth following, she decided. She put the tile in her purse.

They wandered down Leselidze Street in the direction of home. At that time in the early evening, Leselidze was bustling with expats and well-travelled Georgians. Broken and accented English mixed with the sibilant Georgian tongue, punctuated by thick consonants that only a native could pronounce.

Only a few stray passers-by could be heard mumbling in Russian. Irakli invited Teresa to stop at a restaurant called Soko (Mushroom). Soko was below the ground and insulated from the crowds. Inside it was cool and almost deserted, except for a university-aged foreigner huddling alone against the wall, slouching over his laptop, and two middle-aged Georgian women, who had come to complain about their husbands' love affairs.

Like a typical Georgian host, Irakli insisted on treating Teresa to all the varieties of *khachapuri* the restaurant had to offer: *ajaruli* (with an egg); *imeruli* (overflowing with cheese); *ossuri* (with potatoes); and *achma* (layered like a cake), *svanuri* (for the meat eaters). He also ordered *lobio* (beans), *pkhali* (Georgian herbs), *badrijani* (eggplant with pomegranate seeds), and multiple plates of bread, freshly baked in the oven below the ground, and cheese. He offered wine, but she preferred lemonade with tarragon, a Georgian specialty.

Irakli loved to speak. Thankfully for Teresa, he did not require an auditor who listened closely. The sound of his own voice was enough. Teresa's mind was on something—someone, rather—else. When she did pay attention, sometimes translating his Russian and Georgian into English in her head, she learned a lot. Irakli enumerated every book he read as a child, the paradoxes of growing up in the Soviet Union, where everything was forever until it was no more, where literature was legislated and prohibited, suppressed and force-fed.

The conversation turned to poetry. Irakli said he admired anyone who could create beautiful verse. "Without our poets," Irakli said, "Georgia would be nothing."

As if on cue, Teresa recited the six poems she knew by heart from Russia's Silver Age, from Mandelstam and Akhmatova, all the way to Pasternak. As Irakli nodded vigorously, Teresa felt that her passion for the written word had been understood. Could the philologist have understood her love for poetry? she wondered to herself. True, they had deciphered a script, and thereby creating a language together. Yet he had dropped her so easily, as if just by snapping his fingers, or swatting a fly. His causal dismissal made her feel like an insect. Was the mother of his child even literate in the many scripts they shared, let alone in the ones they deciphered?

"That's beautiful," Irakli said after a pause, then added, "As for me, I'm a lover of prose."

Irakli then began to enumerate the socialist realist novels he read as a child, which bore titles like *Cement*, *The Quiet Don*, and *How the Steel was Tempered*. When he read these texts in class, they were taught to him as uncritical celebrations of the Soviet experiment, including collectivization (a Soviet policy that required the landowning class to give up their homes) and the communal apartments that required families to live together, sharing kitchens and bathrooms. But when he brought the novels home, to absorb by candlelight when the rest of the world was sleeping, Irakli discerned a different meaning in each text. In spite of their best intentions to toe the party line, each of these socialist realist authors captured for Irakli the full horror of collectivization and communalization. It was impossible for Irakli to discern in these Soviet fictions the messages he had been schooled to believe in. The paradox, Irakli concluded, was not that so much terrible literature was produced in the Soviet Union, as that the Soviet education system was able to turn so many decent and courageous books into fodder for ideologies that the texts themselves transcended.

When Teresa and Irakli left the restaurant, rain was pounding on the roof. They walked a few blocks before stopping beneath a stone entrance to the French Catholic Church. According to the plaque to the right of the entrance, the church had been erected in 1802, in the very early years of Russian rule, before the colonial regime had had time to erect buildings to celebrate its dominion. That it was now, two centuries later, still in perfect shape meant that someone was paying to have it refurbished. Georgia's visa-free regime was paying off, Teresa mused.

Irakli loved to talk. Whether the subject was politics, the economy, or the future, he could go on forever, so long as the main topic of conversation was Georgia. Teresa didn't mind his loquaciousness. To the contrary, she was grateful: it gave her an excuse for being silent. How I wish you were the philologist, she thought to herself. Now that the philologist turned out to be a husband as well as a father, now that there would be no more deciphering of Sogdian merchant scripts, her imagination reduced him to a symbol of himself, a cipher for a way of living with texts and a way of being textual.

The philologist was a text, a text who aroused her, and who hurt her more intensely than any human could do. Although he was eloquent and erudite, the philologist lacked humanity. Neither as a text nor as a person did he want her in the way she wanted him. And yet, although he was a phantom she had never met, Teresa wanted to be with him more than anyone else in on earth. There was no substitute for his absence. *How I wish you were the philologist I used to love*, Teresa repeated to herself, as Irakli extemporized on Georgian history.

While she was still immersed in thinking about the philologist, Teresa realized that her new companion shared a name with the second-to-last Georgian king, Irakli II. In the closing years of the eighteenth century, Irakli surrendered his country to Russia under great duress. Faced with an impossible choice, of witnessing his beloved Tbilisi ravaged along with the rest of Georgia by the Qajar ruler Agha Mahmed Khan or controlled by the Russians, King Irakli opted for the latter. During the decades that followed, countless Georgian poets reflected on his fatal decision in anguished verse. The Romantic poet Nikoloz Baratashvili died shortly after composing his most famous monument to Georgia's tragic fate: *Bedi kartlisa* ("Georgia's Fate").

After Irakli placed Georgia under Russia's protection in 1795, the country was ravaged to the ground by invading Qajars, just as he had feared. He had hoped to avoid this outcome by annexing Georgia to Russia. The colonial state had been promising for decades to come to Georgia's aid should the Qajars decide to invade, but, when this happened, Russian troops were nowhere to be found. Irakli learned through this bitter experience that he had given up his country's sovereign for nothing. Russian betrayal was to become a pattern in Georgian history, persisting into the present, and poisoning relations between the two countries.

The rain slowed their progress. The hem of Teresa's skirt was soaked but she barely noticed. Irakli continued narrating Georgia's past, summoning to his mind everything he had learned in primary school, as they stood in front of the steel gates facing the church. Women walked past, their black calico skirts drenched. The buckets they carried were covered with wet cloth. Drops of water trickled from their heads to the ground. Irakli was moving backwards in time, bypassing the Safavids and the Mongols and approaching Georgia's medieval period.

"This was Georgia's Golden Age," he explained. He stumbled when he reached the reigns of David the Builder and Queen Tamar.

Finally, Irakli reached the borderland between history and myth, arrived at the legend of Medea. His tone of objective historical narration stopped and he became more personal. According to the Greek version of the myth, Medea was from Colchis, in western Georgia.

"Many Georgian girls are named in honor of this mysterious woman who killed her own sons," he said.

"Do people think she did an honourable thing?" Teresa asked. "By killing her sons?"

"She is remembered fondly because she refused to

permit her children to live in shame with a father who betrayed their mother by marrying another woman.

Teresa kept her silence. She didn't agree with the moral calculus involved in Medea's decision, didn't agree that that it was better for a mother to kill her sons rather than accept the humiliation of being cheated on. *Wouldn't the world be a better place*, she wondered, *if everyone just slept with whomever they want to? What is the purpose of all this shame?*

Irakli seemed to sense her discomfort with his answer. "When you think about it, judging on purely human terms," Irakli added, "she wasn't such a great woman."

"No," Teresa agreed. "But the point isn't whether she was good or bad. Her suffering is shared by all women."

Now Irakli was confused. In less than a minute, Teresa had gone from being appalled at Medea's behaviour to identifying with her. He didn't know anymore what was the right answer. He just knew that he wanted to give the answer that was most pleasing to her. "So now you support Medea?" he asked, afraid that she might be offended by his question, but unsure what else to say.

Teresa smiled. "I sympathize with all women who suffer from jealousy."

Irakli mused, racking his brain for an answer she might like. After a long silence, he gave up, and decided simply to speak his mind. "I think Medea should have been willing to sacrifice her love for her children's happiness."

Teresa was eager for debate. She wanted to contradict him just for the sake of having an argument. Anything to distract her from her grief over the philologist. "It's easy to relate to a woman who will do anything to get revenge."

Irakli continued to stare. What was making her talk like

this? he wondered. A long silence followed, during which the rain pounded harder and harder on the metal grating overhead. Water flowed down the sidewalk. A young boy splashed in a puddle until his mother called his name, and pulled him by the hand.

"Irakli," Teresa finally broke the silence. "Have you ever been in love?"

Irakli closed his eyes and smiled faintly. "Yes," he said. "Once, a long time ago, I was in love with a girl. That was in 1991, right before the Soviet Union crashed. We struck bottom, lost all our money. Our currency was devalued. Most of my friends lost their jobs. Others never received their salaries; the companies they worked for went bankrupt. Many of my friends died of hunger, others of heartbreak. They felt they had no future, nothing left to live for. During those difficult years, that girl I loved had the chance to move to America. Her cousins in New York invited her to stay with them. She left and never returned. I never saw her again."

"Did she love you?" asked Teresa.

"Why do you ask?"

Teresa was still thinking about the philologist. She was measuring Irakli's disappointment in love against her own recent disaster. Surely the philologist never loved her. Did he even care for her at all? Would he have abandoned her like Irakli's beloved, under similar circumstances?

"I don't know," Teresa said. "I was just wondering."

Without answering her question, Irakli continued, "I made a choice after she left for America. I promised myself that I would devote my life to helping my mother. She needed me more at that time than any other woman. Ever since she left, my mother and I have struggled to survive the collapse of the Soviet Union. Only in the last few years have we managed to make a comfortable life that matched our standard of living during the Soviet period. All those years, my mother needed me to work, but most of all she needed me to take care of her. Once she fell and broke her leg. She was hospitalized for a week, and I was the only person who visited her. She doesn't need me so much now. But old habits die hard. I've given up on the other kind of happiness I dreamed about before the Soviet Union fell."

Teresa looked at Irakli. She felt that she was seeing him for the first time. With the sting of the philologist's abandonment still fresh in her memory and etched onto her body, Irakli's words could have been her own.

"We've both given up on finding a partner," she said quietly. "Do you know why birth rates are so low among educated people? Because the more a person learns, the less a person believes in the future. To have children, you have to believe in the future."

Irakli stared back, unsure how to respond. The rain had stopped, but they lingered in front of the gate, lost in reflection. Irakli was the first to break the silence. "Don't mistake me for my namesake," he finally said. "King Irakli should never have surrendered his country to Russia. He had no right to sacrifice the lives of others to protect himself. He should have been willing to die for his country."

"Maybe he just didn't know what he was doing," Teresa said. "If that was the case he would be like a lot of us."

Irakli reflected. "Maybe you're right. But he caused great harm."

"It isn't fair to judge people by the effects of their choices, when they can't know what will result."

Irakli didn't respond. "We'd better set off home," he said. He reached for her hand. With her mind still on the philologist, Teresa placed her hand in his with a passion that surprised her, like an eruption of a volcano everyone had assumed to be dormant.

"You've sacrificed everything, Irakli," Teresa said on the way home. "Do you have any regrets?"

Irakli didn't answer. For once it was Teresa who was the talkative one, and Irakli who remained silent.

They walked down streets haunted by Soviet legacies. Iashvilis Kucha. Besikis Kucha. Griboedovis Kucha. Eseninis Kucha. Each of these streets was named in honor of one of the many poets who had passed an important segment of their life in this city, and where they composed their most important work: Iashvili, Besiki, Griboedov, and Esenin. So many poets had walked these streets shortly before being arrested and carted off to the GULAGs, or worse, tortured and killed. So many poets had risked their lives, their families, their happiness in order to practice their art, to write poems they believed in, and to speak the truth. They were doomed.

They passed a plaque for Paolo Iashvili, who, expecting to be arrested and executed, committed suicide in 1937, and then for Iashvili's best friend Titsian Tabidze, executed the same year, after having been accused of spying for the United States of America. Shortly before he was killed, Titsian cleverly answered the interrogators' demand that he reveal the names of his collaborators by saying he had collaborated with Besiki. He did not tell the interrogators that Besiki was a seventeenth-century Georgian poet, the last great Persianate voice in a world that was being subsumed within another, western-facing, cultural environment. The interrogators scoured Tbilisi in search of the spy whom the accused poet had identified, but no one could tell them where Besiki lived. Both poets, Iashvili and Tabidze, died during the years that they were writing their best works.

"If Medea was wrong to sacrifice her sons, and Irakli was wrong to sacrifice his country, then when it is okay to do something for yourself?" Teresa asked.

"It's okay to do something for yourself when no one else will be hurt, and when the consequences of what you did will be erased the next day," Irakli answered. Teresa wondered to herself if it would ever be possible to join her body with the philologist while abiding by Irakli's strict requirements.

Soon they arrived at the shared courtyard of the apartment where Teresa had been staying for the past month. It fronted a building on Griboedov Street adjacent to Tbilisi's Music Conservatory, and not far from the apartment when Titsian had been living when he was arrested. The Conservatory had been converted from a palatial residence built by a colonial administrator soon after the Russian annexation of Georgia in 1801 into a communal apartment housing twenty families. Her building appeared to have a similar history. Now, a decade and a half after the collapse of the Soviet Union and the end of Soviet-mandated housing, the number of families living there had dwindled to ten. The building's other residents had either died or immigrated to America.

Irakli invited Teresa inside his portion of the communal apartment, on the side of the courtyard opposite her apartment. Beatrice had gone to the countryside with her niece, so the apartment was, for a rare evening, empty of every other human inhabitant.

They sat together talking over tea for a few minutes. It did not take long before conversation yielded to another kind of proximity. His hands lingered on her knee, reminding her of the way he had held her hand as they made their way through the rain-soaked streets of Tbilisi. Then, during a lull in their conversation, he bent over slightly and kissed her cheek. She did not resist.

"Is this okay?" Teresa asked. "Will your mother be upset if she finds out?"

"She would be happy," Irakli smiled. "She's always been telling me that every man needs a woman."

Teresa then recalled Beatrice's wink on Easter evening as she thrust a second egg into her hand. *Was she trying to arrange things*, she wondered, *so that Irakli would be sitting beside me now, his hand in mine, his lips on my chest?*

When their bodies joined, the feeling was somehow predictable to Teresa, and yet in certain ways unexpected. Who would have thought that making love could be so easy, so free of anxiety and expectation, so independent of second guesses, so much about the present?

Having never met the philologist, Teresa lacked a precise sense of his physical appearance. That made it easier for her to project his body onto Irakli's thin frame, as they lay in bed together, breathing heavily in the exhausted afterglow of sex.

Irakli was a nice man, she decided. A bit loquacious, but quite smart, and a sensitive reader of literature. He talked a lot, but he also knew how to listen. He lacked the philologist's genius for deciphering scripts, but he knew all the Soviet classics: Titsian, Iashvili, even Russian writers like Mandelstam. He couldn't recite poetry, but he understood listen to it, which was as important. He had successfully resisted the pressure to become a hypocrite that came with growing up under an oppressive regime. He seemed to have maintained his integrity through it all and not lost his taste for truth. He had resisted Soviet dogma without buying into the clichés of revolutionary transformation that circulated after the Soviet Union's end. And most important of all, he knew how to love a woman. His dedication to his mother was the sign of that.

Unlike the king after whom he was named, Irakli would not betray his family just to protect himself. He had ended his relationships with women when they were constraining his ability to help his mother. For that last feat of generosity, Teresa could have fallen in love with him in other circumstances. But, circumstances being what they were, she did not allow herself to speculate beyond the present.

Teresa kissed every corner of his body, every crevice, contour, and hole. Hair spidered down his legs, mirroring the scarlet columns of veins beneath his skin. The lines captivated her imagination. She traced them with her tongue, all the way down to his toes, which she tenderly kissed. *Did the philologist have black hair like that,* she wondered, *so smooth beneath the touch*?

When Irakli first touched her lips, Teresa had imagined that it was the philologist whose body she was kissing, and that the philologist who was kissing her back. As their kissing became more passionate, and Irakli's hands stroked her body with ever greater intensity, the philologist vanished from her consciousness. She became one with her body, until, suddenly, a few minutes into their lovemaking, her body became one with Irakli's. For a brief five minutes, Teresa was utterly a part of Irakli and utterly alone. The philologist was gone. He was on another planet, peaceful and remote with his wife and newborn baby. They fell asleep, hand in hand, on opposite sides of the bed.

Teresa awoke early the next morning. Her return flight for America was scheduled to depart later that day. Back to the Iowa cornfields, far from Soviet and post-Soviet austerities that haunted Tbilisi. Time to pack. Irakli was deep in sleep, and she did not want to wake him, did not want to make him dwell on the consequences of what their bodies had done to each other. He had enabled her to forget, temporarily, about the philologist and his Sogdian merchant scripts. She kissed his toes in gratitude, softly, so as not to disturb his sleep.

Now Teresa was ready to return to the scripts she had left undeciphered, even if it meant returning alone. She would publish the results of her virtual exchanges, crediting the philologist where credit was due, but otherwise honoring his peaceful exit from her life. These publications would lay the foundation for her future reputation in Sogdian philology. She could then have a career, even though she was not sure she wanted one. She would be grateful to the philologist for helping to launch her career, and would remember fondly the words they exchanged, even when from time to time, she wished that things had turned out differently, that their virtual intimacies had had a physical dimension. She remembered a stanza from W.B. Yeats's poem "When You Are Old," and applied it to herself, to her everlasting, tragic, and unrequited love:

And bending down beside the glowing bars,
Murmur, a little sadly, how Love fled
And paced upon the mountains overhead
And hid his face amid a crowd of stars.

Irakli was now snoring, deep in sleep. Teresa kissed Irakli for a second time, on his forehead. She tiptoed towards the door. He continued to snore. When she reached the kitchen, she opened her purse and fished out the gold-plated tile that had fallen from the faux minarets fronting Old Tbilisi's Blue Bath, that Irakli had advised her to keep for good luck. The tile, she noticed was quite fragile, easy to break. She struck the edge on the rim of the kitchen counter, and it cracked right down the middle, dividing the heart-shaped blue flower in two. She placed one half in her purse, and left the other on the center of the table, clearing a space to make sure Irakli would see it.

Goodbye, Georgia, she thought to herself as she stood on the threshold. *Goodbye, Georgia of ancient myths and magical dream. Goodbye, Sogdian merchant scripts, to which I will only return as to a fragment of my former self, a vestige of a dead civilization, that I exhumed with a man who never loved me.* Then she gently pried open the door and tiptoed out. Irakli continued to snore.

5.

Uneaten Tiramisu

Light spread out over St John the Divine's Cathedral as she stood waiting for him on Amsterdam Avenue, at the intersection of 110th Street, on a dusky afternoon. Although Teresa had lived in this city for many years, on that day she felt as if she were seeing it for the first time, through a stranger's eyes. Morningside Heights was bustling. Workers' eyes brimmed with anger as they headed home from work. It was the wrong time to be waiting for a friend. Their stress clashed with her elation.

Ahmed had never been to the Hungarian Pastry Shop, her favorite spot for meeting friends and prospective lovers alike, so she had offered to wait for him outside. While waiting for him to arrive, she imagined what he might look like as she leaned against the cathedral's cold grey limestone. Its gothic spires towered above her, deflecting the glare of the sun. She had already seen numerous pictures of him, but seeing someone in the flesh often brings with it a surprise.

She passed the time musing how his voice would sound. He had been born in Egypt and was a native speaker of Arabic. Would he have an accent?

Finally, she saw someone who fit his online profile, getting out of a yellow taxi. He paid the driver in cash, and hurried to where she was standing.

Although he did not conform to any stereotype of attractiveness, his trimmed beard and spectacles were charming. His shy smile suggested someone bookish and serious, capable of perceiving layers of meaning beneath action and sign.

She led the way to the café, but he took over as soon as they were inside. He scanned the handwritten menus quickly, as if he had read many such billboards before and knew exactly how to handle them. LEMON SLICE, HAZELNUT SLICE, CHERRY LINZER, APPLE LINZER, AND CHOCOLATE TIRAMISU were inscribed in block letters above the cash register.

"We'll take two tiramisus and two café lattes," he said.

"Your name?" the waiter asked.

"Ahmed."

"Thanks Ahmed. Please take a seat and we'll bring them to your table."

She was surprised that he did ask her what she wanted, although, truth be told, he had guessed her mind: tiramisu and café latte was exactly what she needed.

He spoke as soon as they sat down. "I hope it's ok that I ordered for you? I was thinking you could get something else later if you don't like what I've chosen."

How strange. He seemed to know her taste in food better than she knew herself. "Don't worry about it," she said and smiled, hoping that the awkwardness would pass.

A long silence ensued, punctuated by searching stares and awkward smiles. They had been in touch with each other well for months, although they had never met in person. Tens of thousands of words had been exchanged, in long email chains and WhatsApp messages. These has been followed by hour-long phone conversations, which usually took place when he started work at dawn. He had helped her understand the arcane legal texts that she needed to understand to process divorce proceedings. She could not afford to hire a lawyer on her own. She had given him advice about his son, all over the phone and by email. Now, at long last, they were meeting in the flesh, and did not know what to say to each other.

She decided to begin with distant topics. She had been busy helping a friend from Syria with his asylum application and was now anxiously waiting for him to get a visa.

"The way things are going these days," she said, "I'm not holding my breath." The Muslim ban had just come into effect. Syria was on the list of restricted countries. She hoped against hope that he would be granted a waiver. Surely he deserved special consideration for having been imprisoned and tortured for his resistance to Assad's regime? Perhaps that was too much to hope for from the current government.

He nodded and asked whether she had a personal connection to the Syrian man she was trying to bring to the US. Such a good listener!

"Yes," she said, without missing a beat. His question conveniently displaced her interest in him onto someone far away who could not object to the distortion.

The tiramisu arrived. It was more beautiful than she remembered: two towers of cream, split by layers of dark chocolate shavings and fresh strawberries. Like a wedding cake. Its pure, creamy fluff was so lovely that she was afraid to eat it in front of him. He had no such scruples however, and began cutting his portion with a fork and stuffing his mouth as soon as the waiter set down the plates. When he noticed that she was watching him in a kind of reverie, he explained: "I'm starving. Haven't eaten all day."

He carried the thread of their conversation forward, inviting her to reminisce about her year in Syria, just before the war, learning Arabic in Jami al-Nour, a mosque complex located in Salhiyeh, the neighbourhood where the famous Sufi Ibn al-Arabi is buried. She revealed the shock and disgust of her Sunni landlord when they learned that she was of Shia background. Her fondest memories were of the migrants from the Philippines who cleaned her room and of listening to Bob Marley's "Redemption Song" reverberate on the radio as she coasted along the edge of Salhiyeh with her Iranian friends.

They talked about everything under the sun, everything that was on their minds other than the thing that was staring them in the face: what their future together held. Were they to be friends? Lovers? Strangers who would only meet once and then never see each other again? Why had they agreed to meet, when they could have continued as before, confining their exchanges to email and phone?

They stared at their plates. Only crumbs remained on his plate. Her tiramisu by contrast stood like a tall tower, layered with chocolate, cream, and strawberries. She pushed it gently towards him, inviting him to eat it. He smiled and pushed it back towards her.

"At least eat the chocolate layer," she offered, imagining his lips closing around morsels of her food.

"No," he said. "It's yours."

The clever conversational detours away from the discussion of their future began to frustrate her, but she hesitated to force the topic on him. She steered the conversation in a direction she hoped might inadvertently lead to illumination. She told him about touching the perpetually oversubscribed "Introduction to Islamic Civilization" survey course to Columbia undergraduates. The students' favoritereading was by the Egyptian Sayyid Qutb, who passed much of his life in prison and became an inspiration for the Muslim Brotherhood. In the selection chosen for class, Qutb argued that polygamy was a more natural state for women and men than monogamy. She recounted how one woman in her class praised the article for its realism and honesty and said it made her to think differently about woman's sexuality. She said she disagreed with large parts of it, but it had stimulated her thinking.

Her tiramisu lingered between them, obstructing their access to each other, two towering slices criss-crossed by layers of mascarpone cheese, cocoa-flavoured cream, and lady fingers dipped in coffee. She moved her fork through the cake, savouring its moist texture, and anticipating its touch on her tongue. But for whatever reason she could not bring it to her lips. She wondered what it would be like to feed him a morsel from the tower of tiramisu, to watch his lips slowly close around the heaps of dark chocolate, the ripe strawberries, and the cocoa-flavored cream.

She did not let her mind linger on these images for long. She reminded herself of the dangers they involved and was not even sure she wanted to experience intimacy with him. He was a good friend, a sincere supporter, and a trusty source of advice and support in times of need. Why ruin all that with a fling? Rather than destroying their friendship, she wanted to transform it into something more lasting, more intimately connected to the core of her being. She had been reading recently about men and women who decided to break with monogamy's norms and have multiple romantic partners. She decided to introduce the subject into their conversation elliptically, by discussing a film about William Moulton Marston, the creator of the Wonder Woman comic strip, who lived in a three-way partnership with two women. She asked him whether he had seen it.

"No," he said, "is there a reason why I should?"

She didn't know how to answer his question, so she hedged. "Yes," she said, "it might teach you something about love." She wanted to go into more detail, to describe the three-way love affair between the characters in the movie, but she was filled with shame.

Carrying the conversation about the filmed further seemed too risky. She decided to change topics. Philosophy. As a lawyer with an unquenchable appetite for analysis, surely Ahmed would be interested in what Bertrand Russell had to say on the topic of married relations.

"Have you read Bertrand Russell's *Marriage and Morals*?" she asked him.

"No," he responded as he had to the film, "Is there a reason why I should?"

"Yes. It's a brilliant critique of the patriarchal institution of marriage and an argument for non-monogamy."

She couldn't summon the courage to use the word "poly" or any of its variants, but she was hoped that the discussion had impressed on him the fluidity of the boundaries between love and friendship. That was all she could hope to do really: extend possibilities, plant questions in his mind.

He stared at her in silence. His eyes were sparkling, and gave her courage. She decided to steer the conversation in the direction she needed most: "Tell me about your wife."

Ahmed smiled the brightest smile he had smiled that day.

"My wife is the most amazing woman in my life," he said, and launched into a paean of her intelligence, her integrity, and her sense of humour. He explained how she had agreed to have two children, now aged five and ten, only with reluctance, and on the condition that he would do the child rearing himself. They arranged the workload carefully: she kept her full-time job working as a curator for the Met's South Asian galleries, while he reduced his hours at his firm and work from home. He took the children to school every morning, and she picked them up only when it fit in with her work schedule. Then he began recollecting what she was like when they met, and when he fell in love with her. He spoke of her lovers, prior to their marriage, of her insatiable passions, the intensity of her desires.

The more he told her about his wife, the more she saw in her an image of herself. He pulled out his wallet and showed a picture of the four of them—wife, five-year old son, ten-year old girl, and himself—atop Mt. Kilimanjaro. He then pulled out his phone and began flipping through other images: of her coming home from work, of them walking the streets of London, Amsterdam, and Madrid.

It was uncanny: his wife looked like her too. Like her, she was tall and red-haired, with glasses and curls that reached to her shoulders. She liked to wear long, loose-fitting dresses, and she could see from the pictures of her travelling the world that neither of them liked to wear makeup. As he breathlessly summarized her passions, she felt that she resembled his wife in personality too: they were both voracious readers, incessant questioners, and insatiable curators of the life of the mind.

The plate of her uneaten tiramisu came into view again. She found herself dreaming about sharing tiramisu with his wife, just as she had been dreaming about intimacy with him, eating his tiramisu, just a few minutes earlier. Of spooning the layers of chocolate and cream into her mouth and her savouring every bite.

Speaking of his wife bought a flash of light to his face, and the conversation became more animated. He told her of how they met her while they were working at the UN, how he fell in love with her for her toughness and her brilliance, how he proposed marriage to her while they were vacationing in Thailand, and persuaded to her to have children. They signed a strict prenuptial agreement, in order to insure that they relationship was always governed by reason. The more she learned about this woman, the more Teresa liked her. She was tough and resilient. Perhaps, Teresa wondered, his life is even more interesting than he is.

The conversation tapered to an end. The sun had set nearly half an hour ago. Lone yellow cabs were lined up along the sidewalks. Other than that, the streets were deserted.

"Time to go home," he said softly, with a bashful smile on his face, and began gathering his things. She nodded assent and rose to leave. It seemed that his hand grazed hers as he cleaned the table but she was not sure.

She imagined him greeting his wife, and them locked in a passionate embrace that she wanted to be a part of too.

He then paused and stared deep into his eyes, as if seeking for something memorable to say, something that would not be filled with falsehood: "this sure didn't go like we expected, did it?"

She wanted to ask what he meant, but shame filled her again, along with fear. She decided not to probe further, to just leave his query as a rhetorical question.

Finally, the moment for parting approached. She wanted to make it memorable, wanted to move their relationship forward in some way, wanted for the hours they had just spent together not to be in vain. She wanted the experience of multiple love, not a crude sexual liaison of a threesome, but actual love: a powerful and passionate three-way relationship, between her and a man and also a woman, motivated and consumed by love.

"Can you introduce me to your wife?" she finally asked. Their relationship was entering new, unchartered terrain. She did not know where it would lead, but she did know that life was short. A new horizon seemed to be opening in front of them, between her and Ahmed, and then, among the three of them: her, Ahmed, and his wife.

What was it that she wanted from this woman, the wife of the man she had just begun to fancy as a lover? She didn't know. She had a feeling, however, that the bond that might emerge from that union would be stronger than her magnetic attraction for the man in front of her. But first he had to introduce them to each other. And they both had to agree to a three-way relationship, founded in love.

"Why do you want to meet her?" he asked, surprised. "I thought we met here so that you and I could get to know each other."

"She sounds amazing," she said. "Just like the kind of woman whom I'd want to have in my life, with whom I could fall in love. I thought she might be able to teach us both something about love."

"Are you a lesbian?" he asked in confusion.

She smiled, and, instead of an answer, touched his cheek gently with the palm of her hand.

"Nothing as simple as that—" she began. Her voices trailed off, as she could not figure out how to end the sentence.

As they stood up to leave, she noticed that the uneaten tiramisu still lingered on her plate. She hated to think of it thrown away, mixed in with all the gross substances in a trash can, when it was such a work of beauty, so sweet to the taste. She asked their waiter to pack it up. When he brought it back, neatly wrapped in white Styrofoam, she handed it to Ahmed. "Please give this to your wife," she said. "Tell her it's a gift from me, from me, this tiramisu, ordered by you, who seems to know what I want better than I know myself."

6.

The Breakdown of Love

I.

"You must tell me if you ever feel unloved," he whispered as he ran his fingers through her hair. They had known each other for only three days, yet something extraordinary had happened. They had lived through the process before, and were wary of releasing the familiar aphrodisiacs into the air. Their flesh was heavy with the smells, tastes, and memories of former affections.

"If you ever feel unloved, you will tell me, ok?"

"Ok," she said.

"Promise?"

She promised, unable to imagine feeling unloved by him, the most affectionate man she had ever known. For the past six days, his hands had been fixed to some part of her body. They had met in Paris, in arrondissement 13, at the Hotel Belambra on Rue Corvisart. They had been introduced to each other by one of his friends, Sam, who was trying to help Demetrious break with his past. Sam had met Teresa at the memorial service for her husband, who had died three years earlier in a car crash. Although she would never forget him, she told Sam over too many glasses of wine, she was ready to move on, to find another man. The problem was that there was no one to fall in love with, no one not already committed, no one whom she could stand or trust.

"Well," said Sam, "I have a friend in the same situation, also looking for love."

Sam's friend was a Greek man named Demetrious, father of one. He was a recent divorcée. Demetrious was also a friend of one of her friend Jessica. Hence they were connected by two degrees of separation. Sam told Demetrious that his friend had a friend whom he should meet. "She's in your same situation," he said, smiling suggestively.

"You're a match made in heaven," Jessica whispered in Teresa's ear as she escorted her to the train station. "I predict you'll be drawn to each other and will never let go."

Had she been given a selection of men to choose from, he would not have been her first choice. He was a civil servant in the vast bureaucracy of the European Union, and a theoretical physicist by training. What could be less promising than a man who had no practical use or need for art? She had had her fill of scientists in her private life. Her father had been a failed mathematician, and he had made her childhood miserable with endless compulsory lessons in calculus. As a category, scientists, especially male ones, struck her as emotionally tepid, narrow-minded, vulgar, and unable to speak about anything not directly relevant to their field of expertise.

Even worse: he had abandoned his research after receiving his PhD. So he entered the civil service, binding his future to the state. A bureaucrat! A sell-out! How could they possibly connect? His job brought in a good income and job security, but it could never give his life meaning. Her vocation paid badly, and sometimes made her miserable, yet her work enriched the meaning of her existence. *What if he hates what I love?* she mused. *Or hates the fact that I love them? What if he's intimidated by me, as men tend to be?* Notwithstanding her doubts, Teresa agreed to meet him in Paris. She lived in the UK, so it had to involve a weekend journey.

II.

When she arrived at the hotel, she rang him up at the reception. He came down to meet her. They greeted each other like old friends. Breakfast extended into lunch. Lunch soon became a dinner they dreamed would last forever. The conversation stretched like a train traversing the mountains, full of possibilities, with no end in sight. They had so much to say! Demetrious could not summon the courage to kiss her on the first night, although he wanted to. He pecked her goodnight and they parted to their separate rooms.

She stayed up late that night, excited. Her skin felt as if it was being pricked by needles, in an oddly pleasurable way. Something was about to happen, to her, to him, to their lives. She appreciated the delay; it gave her time to savour the anticipation, and to wait for his kiss. It only goes downhill after that, she told herself, weary and jaded with memories of the past lovers from her pre-marriage years.

Early on the morning of their second day together, immediately after breakfast, he asked if he could come to her room. He started telling her about a novel he was reading, *Stoner* by John Williams, an American novel from the 1960s that had been neglected during the author's lifetime and forgotten until its recent rediscovery, in a French translation, in 2013. Teresa was intrigued by Demetrious' European take on American fiction, as he rehearsed the novel's plot. Then suddenly, he stopped in mid-sentence and kissed her on the lips. From that moment onwards, her body felt in one way or another grafted to his.

After the breakfast that became a kiss, they continued talking all through the afternoon and deep into the night. They canvassed the city, oblivious to their surroundings. After hours of walking along the Seine, they arrived at Shakespeare & Co, the bookstore that had hosted Joyce and Hemingway. They entered. Every time one of them saw a book on the shelf that they had read, they turned and asked whether the other had read it. Then they sat closely together on a dilapidated sofa in the back room on the second story, reading the titles off the shelves one by one from their intimate position.

They spent two days wandering around the catacombs and in and out of the Pantheon. The alleys and boulevards of Paris were recast in the images of their beloved writers, poets, and filmmakers. Rue Lepic became the plays of Chekhov. Rue Saint-Antoine were absorbed into the novels of Dostoevsky. Rue des Rosiers merged with the films of Krzysztof Kieślowski. As they meandered down narrow alleys, he invited her to travel back with him to Brussels, to pass the rest of the vacation with him in his recently acquired home.

"My house is huge!" he exclaimed. "I'll create a room just for you for when you want to be alone."

It was winter vacation for them both. His son was spending the break with his mother, so they could extend their date across the entire Christmas holiday and celebrate the New Year together. They celebrated that decision—and their acquaintance—that night over champagne.

"2015 has been a year of partings and deaths," Teresa said, "Here's to hoping that 2016 will be a year of union."

They took the Thalys train from Paris to his Brussels home, their legs pressed against each other for the entire journey. The sensation of touching anyone in that way, with unabating intensity and ever increasing intimacy, was a distant memory for them both. The first thing he showed her when they arrived was his three oak bookshelves, carved into the wall, filled with an assortment of DVDs, Blu-rays, and even old videos.

"I built them myself," he said with pride. "I like to build my own shelves for storing my most valuable possessions."

His collection of films and of books was vast, covering all times, places, and genres. He admitted that he had not read most of the books, but he said he had seen most of the films, sometimes many times. On the opposite wall was a small library of books about film, organized by country.

The third row of the middle shelf was dedicated to the films of his favoritedirector, Fritz Lang. Demetrious told her about Lang's escape to Hollywood during the Third Reich, on the day he'd been offered the position of head of the national German film studio by Joseph Goebbels himself. Lang's wife refused to accompany her husband and chose instead to remain behind with the Nazi regime.

"What do you say we organize a mini-film festival in honour of your arrival?" he suggested. "To celebrate New Years, 2016?"

She smiled as he wrapped his arms around her. "You're always full of brilliant ideas."

"Is that a yes?" he asked, and kissed her on the lips.

She kissed him back. His tongue dug into her mouth, and soon they were passionately making love on the sofa.

The improvised film festival was to be held in the basement, which doubled as a screening room. On the first night, they watched two films, one from Lang's German period and one from after his migration to America. During the second film, while they were both fully clothed, she gently caressed his penis until it was entirely erect. It became a pattern. Sometimes they would continue watching the movie to the end, and sometimes they would stop right in the middle of the film and make love.

The night when he insisted that she tell him if she ever felt unloved was the third day of the film festival. M from the German period had been followed by You Only Live Once from Lang's American era. They ate *bougatsa*, a cream-filled Greek pie, together, licking the lemon sauce topping off each other's lips.

They went to bed that night as they had done on each of their days in Paris: in each other's arms, with her head tucked into his chest. He woke up sweating, wrapped his arms even more tightly around her, and wrapped his legs around hers. The combination of conversation and physical intimacy brought tears to her eyes. Her body had hungered for such contact for too many years.

On the fourth night of the festival, they switched from Fritz Lang to Demetrious' second favoritedirector, Lars von Trier. The first film they watched, Nymphomaniac, took three full nights to watch because it kept getting interrupted by their passionate lovemaking.

Soon after she was widowed, she had fallen in love with a married man who had not loved her back. When she told him of her feelings, he said, in somewhat mechanical fashion, that his affections were elsewhere. Nothing she could do, he informed her, would ever change that. She was ashamed to admit it, but it was true: her feelings for a married man who had not loved her back had devastated her even more than the death of her husband and the end of her thirteen-year marriage. During these same years, Demetrious had been raising a child with a woman who revealed suddenly, one month before giving birth, that she wanted a divorce. She explained that she had stopped loving him. On the day when she gave birth, she repulsed his embraces and told him she hated the sound of his voice. Teresa's hunger for bodily contact was balm to him on a wound he had been nursing for too long. Several times amid their lovemaking he found himself on the verge of tears.

After they had catalogued all the novels, plays, and short stories they had ever read, she asked him about the poets. "Aren't there any poets you love to read?" she said. "About poetry, you will have to teach me," he answered. "It's a mystery to me why people devote themselves so intensely to this art. Poetry is like gardening. It doesn't do any harm. But what good does it do? Who needs it?"

His indifference to poetry revealed a gap that grew with every conversation. His tone-deadness to the muse placed him at the extreme end of the spectrum of her lovers. Even Irakli whom she had bonded with briefly in Tbilisi, had loved poetry, and Mehdi, whom she had loved for longer in Damascus, recited the poetry of others as if it were his own.

Words were her life, and poetry her sustenance. She felt a twinge of pain as he spoke, as if when he trivialized poetry he also trivialized her. But her discontent soon became submerged with other emotions as they indulged their shared passions.

Five days into her stay in Brussels, she found herself repeating the same verse every day, as if it were a mantra, or a piece of sacred scripture:

This is as close to paradise as it gets,
as much like Eden as the earth permits.

At first the first occurred to be spontaneously, while she was shaving her armpits in the shower. Then it became a mantra that she repeated in the hopes that by pronouncing it many times and in the right way, she would make it true. After a yearlong drought in her emotional existence, she had rediscovered the meaning of love. Now she was afraid that it would slip through her hands, gossamer-like. She feared discovering that she had never really owned this magical emotion, had never fully held it in her grip. Yet she needed to believe in this love, in order to maintain her will to live.

III.

The Brussels interlude was a beautiful rupture in the fabric of time. It passed quickly. Her heart could not bear its intensity, but it lasted long enough to change her world, and to list her up from her grief. She went home to Exeter, a small ancient city in southwest England where she had moved three months earlier in order to take up a position at the local branch of Arts Council English. It was a good temporary job, to keep her busy in between careers. Back in Exeter, she resumed her day-to-day tasks: reviewing grant applications, updating the website with community-sourced poetry about local sites and monument, and scheduling public events. Every week that she passed in

Exeter, she regretted that she living three hours from London, where she felt she most belonged. At first, when Sam died, and she decided to sell their home in the Iowa cornfields and to leave the US forever, it made sense to relocate to a small town rather than a sprawling metropolis. She had to get away from the world, and find a way to work on herself. Now that she was recovering from her grief and meeting new people, she was feeling increasingly confined by the small town-lifestyle of this quaint English town. In spite of its charming antiquity, its white shop windows, and towering medieval cathedral, Exeter was provincial and narrow. It was a town that made foreigners feel like exotic anomalies, wild caged animals. In addition, the Eurostar travelled directly from London to Brussels, placing her in greater proximity to her beloved.

Weeks became months. They spoke every night, for at least an hour, recounting every moment of their divided, compartmentalized lives. How they slept, what they ate, what they wore, the commute to and from work, the minutiae of conversations with co-workers, family, and friends: everything was shared, until, inevitably, certain details began to be slowly, but systematically, omitted, at least on her side. The parts she omitted tended to be those most revealing of her inner life. That life mattered less to him than did the places where she shopped, the number of hours she spent teaching, what she ate for lunch, and the make of the refrigerator in which she stored her food. Unlike with Demetrious, she did not relish sharing such trivialities. With every hour of interrogation, she felt increasingly alienated from the man she wanted to love, who had managed to stop the passage of time with her in Brussels just a few months earlier.

He called her every day. She never called him but she couldn't summon the courage to refuse to take his calls. She knew how important they were to him. He wanted to "do things together," as he put it, and daily phone conversations were a necessary element in this togetherness. Besides, she valued his loyalty. It was better to have too much than too little of that. So she complied with his demands on her patience and time, and didn't allow herself to recognize its negative impact, even within the privacy of her own mind.

As a result of suppressing her feelings, she came to dread their nightly conference calls even more than she dreaded office meetings with her boss. At least her boss knew when to declare the meeting over. Demetrious lacked this ability to bring things to an end. He talked forever, distracted by the hum of his own voice. She lost sleep while forcing herself to think of what she would say to him the next time they spoke. She began to dread his calls. But she did not want to threaten their relationship at such an early stage of gestation. She also worried that she might come to regret distancing herself from the one person in her life who felt the need to talk to her on a daily basis, whether or not she enjoyed it.

After three weeks of such strained exchanges, and partly to introduce a new rhythm to their interactions, she proposed that they reconvene in London. She had a training course coming up on the topic of engaging with government, and the National Theatre was staging a French play that had received rave reviews, called "The Father." An avid playgoer, Demetrious was eager to see it. He bought his Eurostar tickets and requested a few days of leave from work for the beginning of the week. She changed the hotel booking to double occupancy. It was the Park Plaza, a four-star hotel on the south bank of the Thames. She asked for a room with a view of the river. Demetrious booked a separate cheaper hotel for them for the night prior in Hampstead Heath. They spoke with anticipation about this second rendezvous, hoping it would revive the passion that had sprung between them while in Paris and which had followed them to Brussels, until it petered as they tried to maintain the relationship over the phone.

Just as for their first meeting in Paris, she arrived two hours late. She had missed the train, and the next one was delayed. On the journey to London, she had told herself that her delay wouldn't matter much. He would be able to go directly to their hotel, and they would meet there instead of in the centre of London as planned. She had underestimated his patience. He greeted her complaining about the hours he had lost with his son as a result of her tardiness. She tried to soothe his wounds by touching him tenderly in the places that triggered a reaction from his body, while they were in Paris and Brussels. He turned away from her violently.

The night they spent together was full of acrimony. The thrill of being together that had made her skin tingle as they made love in Paris seemed to be lost forever. *Have we stopped loving each other?* She wondered.

The first challenge was deciding where to eat. Every restaurant that appealed to her was too low-class for him.

"You're so cheap!" He said. "You have no appreciation for the good things in life!"

Finally, in order to mitigate the conflict, she decided to agree to any restaurant. After all, he had come to London to see her, and she didn't want to spoil his visit.

Her silence made him even angrier.

"I'm going," he said.

"Going where?" she asked in fear.

"Just going!" he said. "Stop asking questions!"

She reached out, instinctively to touch him, but withdrew when she saw his eyes flare up in anger. What had she done wrong? She trailed him distantly as he raged down the streets. They past Tottenham Court station, perpetually under construction.

"Don't look at me," he screamed. "Your face disgusts me!"

He is right, Teresa thought to herself, *I am irritated by his presence.* She was beginning to grow afraid of his screams and verbal abuse, and the violence it might lead to. Finally, she gave up. *Better just to let go*, she told herself, already in mourning a second time.

Above all they needed a break from each other, even if only a few minutes just so he could quell his rage. "I'll meet you at the theatre entrance at a quarter past seven," she yelled at him, hoping he would hear.

The show started at 7:30. To her surprise, he arrived on time, at 7:15, apparently recovered from his rage. His face was blank, but at least his voice was calm. He gently, if mechanically, grasped her hand.

As they mounted the stairs to their seats, she wondered to herself: *Where did it go, that passion for him that was going to change my life? What made it die?*

The play was short and intense. It told the story of an aging man stricken with Alzheimer's. Each time the father saw his daughter it was as if she were a different person, partnered with a different man. The situation deteriorated with every new scene.

By the end of the play the daughter decided to transfer her father to a nursing home in Paris. She promised to visit, but the viewer could see from her busy life that that was unlikely to happen. Before she parted with her father forever, she promised to visit him every week from London.

Demetrious and Teresa sat in the front row. They held hands throughout the entire play, in spite of the coldness of their palms. Teresa became tense with fear when the play ended because it meant that they would have to start speaking again. She feared that silence would reveal that they had run out of words, not just in that instant but for all time. Three months of love, going on four, and they had nothing left to say to each other.

After the show ended, they filed out and stopped for a quick dinner at Jamie Oliver's, an upscale Italian restaurant just around the corner.

They survived dinner without an argument but only by constantly censoring their thoughts. Their Paris romance seemed a distant dream, a symbol of the passion that they once felt for each other would could not be kindled again. The train was crowed with couples in love, returning from the theatre, or from dancing, but they did not hold hands on the tube ride back to the hotel. Every word seemed to poison the evening air. Teresa decided it was best not to speak at all, less her words instigate another outburst from Demetrious. They kept silent while walking, with several inches between their bodies. The Thames flowed sadly beneath them as they walked past the National Theatre, and crossed Waterloo Bridge. Even the cast iron sphinx at the end of the bridge did nothing to uplift her spirits. How unlike their first night together, which they spent, hand in hand, walking along the Seine!

They fell to sleep on opposite sides of the bed. It was the first sexless night they had spent together over the three months of their acquaintance. When Demetrious started snoring, she rolled over and faced him: "I want to tell you something," she whispered in his ear.

His snoring ceased. He turned away from her. "What?"

"I fantasize about other men when I masturbate. I can only have an orgasm when I think of men other than you."

He pulled away from her slightly and was silent for a long while. Finally, he asked: "Why did you tell me that?"

"I'm worried what this means for us."

He turned his entire body away from her and was soon snoring so loudly that she had to cover her head with a pillow to mute the sound of his mucus blocking the air. She wondered whether he was just pretending to be asleep in order to avoid talking to her, to evade the problems in their relationship, to avoid facing the breakdown of their love.

IV.

They awoke the next morning uncertain how they would spend their day together. London theatres were closed on Sunday. How would they distract themselves from their growing contempt for each other? After arguing for an hour in bed about where to go, they finally agreed on simply exploring the city. She was unsure it was a wise choice because it left open too much space for further arguments, but at least they would be leaving their hotel room, which was beginning to cause claustrophobia.

They walked through Hampstead and up along St. John's Wood to Maresfield Gardens. Unexpectedly, they ended up in front of the house where Sigmund Freud had spent his final years after leaving Vienna, and his daughter Anna had passed the remaining decades of her life. A plaque announced the house as the Freud Museum, open seven days a week. The museum would have excited her on any other occasion, but Demetrious' tense presence, and the feeling of hostility between them, prevented her from enjoying herself. Every moment they passed together seemed to release new toxins into the air, and to further relegate their memories of Paris and Brussels to the distant past. They walked back to the tube in silence.

Then came the battle over where to eat dinner. Finally, he burst out with a critique delivered at high decibel. "All you care about is your career and money!" he shouted. "I've had enough! I'm through!"

He stomped away, leaving Teresa watching him, her jacket wrapped tight around her suddenly diminished body. She felt small and defenceless. Returning to the hotel at night alone was a frightening prospect but it had to be done. As she moved forward into the night, she tried to persuade herself that their argument was a blessing in disguise. To say that they were getting on each other's nerves would have been a wild understatement. Hatred was simmering beneath the surface of their words, waiting to explode in violence. They were driving each other crazy, and were more miserable together than apart. Simple decisions, like where to have dinner, put them on the edge. Every argument generated more anger, and it increasingly seemed like the only way they could get along was by not speaking to each other at all.

When he entered their hotel room around eleven that night, she turned her face towards the window and opened her laptop. He sat down on a corner of the bed and set about searching through his email while she typed feverishly. Thirty minutes passed with them both transfixed by their computers.

Finally, he said: "Can you please stop typing? I need to get some sleep."

She kept punching the keys with her fingertips. He stood and repeated his words. She continued typing. He stared at her for thirty seconds, as if waiting for her to stop, and then lunged towards her, threatening to destroy her laptop.

"I'm gong to call the police and tell them to remove you by force!" he screamed. "This is my room," he insisted. "I paid for it with my credit card! I'll kick you out onto the street!" He continued yelling as she kept her eyes glued to the laptop screen. "You look just like a horse, with your ugly eyes fixed straight ahead of you, never noticing what happens around. Wake up, you selfish bitch!"

He concluded the diatribe by announcing: "It's finished. Meeting you was the biggest mistake of my life. I'm booking a room and leaving you alone tonight. I'm saying goodbye. Have a good life."

She was in shock. She could not conjure within herself the feelings she thought she was supposed to feel when breaking up. She couldn't recall what it felt like to meet him for the first time. She couldn't compel herself to fear his absence from her life. Instead: she became consumed with practicalities: *What will I do when he is gone from my life?* she wondered. She thought about her books. *How will I return them to Exeter? Will I have to have to hire a moving company? Will he ship them back?* Finally, the flow of logistics questions was replaced with a bigger, practical question that she could not answer: *Do I love him? How can I know? What is love? He's forcing me to break up with him.*

Demetrious continued to shout at her. He seemed to take pleasure in insulting her, and to see himself as a kind of truth-teller. What she saw was different. She had seen it before in her father. It was abuse, pure and simple. Although he had thankfully not struck her in the way her father did, the words he was saying to her were words that could never be forgotten. *Why,* she wondered, *do men have such a predilection for violence? What makes them think they can find fulfilment in this way?*

She occupied herself with such thoughts rather than follow his crazed tirade. She played mute, until, growing tired and needing sleep, she finally interrupted him: "You love insulting me."

The words sounded hopelessly weak as soon as they escaped her mouth. Her timidity could not compete with his aggression. Then she realized that, in the heat of argument, what mattered was less what one said that how loudly one could say it. This was a game she did not want to play. She receded into her shell and turned away.

Finally, he fell silent. She approached him in bed. They fell together into a drowsiness that augured the beginning of sleep. She tried touching the backside of his knees, as a kind of experiment, to see whether he had really meant what he said, and whether he was serious about breaking up. He remained still. She could not tell whether this was because he was sleeping or whether he had really intended to end their relationship. She would have liked to know the answer. *Even if he didn't intend to break up,* she reasoned, *even if he thinks we can be together after this argument, it's over. It must be over, if I respect myself. Staying with him would mean accepting his violence. He has a talent for turning love into abuse. I am no masochist. I must refuse.*

When they woke up on Monday, the next morning, she began packing. She was moving to the Park Plaza on the other side of London, booked by the training organization. He could stay as long as he wanted—alone—in the hotel where they were now. They were on the verge of a break-up.

She packed while he fiddled away on his laptop, on the pretence of booking night for himself in the hotel, alone. When she had finished packing and sat down next to him thirty minutes later, he seemed to have made no progress with his booking. What was preventing him? Did he stand by the words he had hurled at her the night before?

She could not say. When she sat down next to him, he looked at her calmly, his deer-brown eyes gaping open, seething innocence. It was impossible to associate them with the violence of last night. These were the eyes she fell in love with in Paris, and then again in Brussels: gentle as a deer, soft, and open to anything and anyone. They were empty of acrimony. She wished she had never had to witness his eyes in any other way.

They lay down together and talked. The conversation covered world events—the Iranian elections, Brexit, the US Presidency—all the while avoiding the events of the night before. Then they touched. He took off his clothes. They made love as they had done in Paris and Brussels, as if nothing and no one existed at that moment outside each other's bodies.

"I want you to have an orgasm," he whispered in her ear. "Coming with me inside you is your task. I won't come until you do."

When they finished, he wrapped his arms around her and said "Let's go to your hotel." The argument from the night before receded into the shadows, like a dream.

That night, for the first time she had arrived in London, they didn't argue about where they would eat. They had lunch at a sushi place nearby, just off Russell Square, and then went to Skoobs, London's largest used bookstore. Here they did exactly as they had done in Paris, the city where their love was born. They skimmed the shelves for books, comparing notes along the way, asking each other for advice on what to buy, and making lists of the many hundreds of books they wanted to read. While engaged in this activity, they seemed made for each other: the world's two most impassioned book collectors. It was like Paris all over again, except with greater familiarity and an ache from the pain of the night before, wounds that we slowly festering for Teresa. Her grief over her husband had by now absorbed this second wound, and she did not see herself healing during her lifetime.

They had almost given up on finding a production for that evening when Demetrious suggested that they look at the playlist for the Almeida Theatre, off West End and in the heart of the Angel district. Demetrious checked online. Uncle Vanya was on that evening. Two seats were available, both behind a thick pillar.

"At least we'll be able to sit together," he said brightly. Chekhov had brought them together while they were walking through Paris, and now, he hoped, he would bring them together again, in London. She called the theatre and booked their seats.

The performance had been negatively reviewed in *The Guardian* due to it its length, but she didn't care. She loved

Chekhov. *The longer the better*, she thought to herself. *Plus, this might be the last time we will ever be together, acting as if we are in love.* They rushed to the theatre hand in hand, and sat down behind the pillars. He whispered to her between the acts, praising the acting. She nodded vigorously to every word he said. He bought ice cream for them both, extravagant as always, two cups each, four flavors: salted caramel, raspberry, vanilla, and hazelnut.

She could tell how pleased he was with the performance by the way he leaned back in his chair, his deer-brown eyes awash in peace. After the show, there was a question-and-answer session with the actors. They sat through it quietly, holding each other's hands. Desire was engulfing them again, turning the violence of the preceding night into a dream and giving their reunion the appearance of reality. The real and the imaginary had become inverted, thanks to Chekhov.

"One thing I always notice about Chekhov's plays," Demetrious said during a brief pause in the question and answers, "is that the characters are always in love with the wrong people. Whether it's Sonya and Michael or Vanya and Elena, these people don't know what's good for them, so they end up hurting themselves."

When the question and answer session ended, he stared deep into her eyes and then kissed her. It was the first time they had kissed in that way since Paris, the first time they had forgotten their surroundings, and the sweetness lingered on her lips. Yet she never forgot that she would have to bring her passion to come to an end, for the sake of her self-preservation. She could not allow herself to be further abused, or to risk further abuse. Even if they saw each other again, for example if she had to pick up her belongings, it would never mean what it had meant before. They would be strangers to each other, just like they were when they kissed in Paris.

They lived through the birth and death of love. Any feelings that might return would always be mingled with that night of acrimony and hate. The hate that had become real for the first time the night before changed everything. Violence had introduced a new dynamic into their relationship. Staying with him after that could mean harm.

They returned immediately to the hotel, hungry for each other's body. It turned out that the view was of a Ferris wheel, not the Thames, but that didn't matter. They spent that night together naked, intimate, free of all strain. As he had done earlier that day, he insisted that she had to orgasm first, and refused to come until she did. He did not want sex just for the sake of his pleasure, he said. He wanted to become part of her sexual fantasies, for her to dream of him only, and not of any other man.

When they had slept together in the past, she would usually lay by his side for an hour until he fell asleep. Then she would go to the restroom or another adjoining room where she would work for a few hours longer on her laptop, often until dawn. She could only work in isolation, far away from him, even if it meant passing the night sitting on the toilet. Then, once the sun began to shine, she would set her alarm, return to bed, and finally fall asleep, after he had already turned his back to her.

This night was different. It was the last night they would spend together. She wanted every moment to last. She did not go to the bathroom, and consequently did not set her alarm. Instead, she fell asleep in his arms.

They woke up two hours late. He had missed his train. She had missed the first session in her training course. Following an initial wave of panic, she realized that she would not be able to say farewell with the tender gestures she had dreamed while falling asleep in his arms on the preceding night. By the time she opened her eyes he was already hunched over his laptop, searching frantically for a new ticket on the Eurostar back to Brussels. From past experience with him in stressful situations, she knew that it was better not to speak. She picked up her bag, whispered: "See you soon," and simply left. She had avoided the awkwardness of parting by not saying goodbye. But it was a lie. She knew she would never see him again. She also knew that he had not understood.

Now, at long last she was alone. A new chapter of her life was opening before her. She relished her solitude and wondered if it might last until her death.

For most of the walk to Euston station she stared at the ground, afraid of what she would see if she lifted her eyes. The sight of young lovers at the edges of her vision was particularly painful. "Love," she said aloud, "What a joke."

The performance the night before had stirred memories of all her past encounters with Chekhov. She loved Chekhov's plays, but she knew his stories even better. One story in particular was etched into her consciousness, so many time had she read it, at different stages of her life. She first encountered "Lady with a Lapdog," during her first year at the university. The story resonated at many different levels, even though she had never had an affair of the kind Chekhov's described between Gurov and Anna Sergeevna. What struck her most about the story was its division between real life, conducted under the cover of night and in secret, and fake life, which defines our work days, our professional relations, everything we do in daylight hours. Most of the world only knows about the second half, even when we mentally inhabit the first. For Chekhov's hero Gurov, real life took place only when he was with Anna. Yet their love was burdened by duplicity: it contravened society's laws and violated conventional morality. He was cheating on his wife, betraying his marriage. When she arrived at Euston Station, Teresa decided to read "Lady with a Lapdog" again. Even if the story could not tell her what to do next, it would help her to face the breakdown of her love with Demetrious.

V.

As Teresa waited for the train that would take her to the training course, she reflected on the catastrophic holiday she had spent—or rather, squandered—with Demetrious. *Why do we hurt the ones we love?* she asked herself, feeling like character in a Chekhov play. *Why do we insult them in ways we would never insult strangers? How can words be so full of hate?*

She boarded the first car, searched for a vacant seat, and sat down. The italics in her head seemed to her to mark the birth of a story. About what precisely, she did not know, but she guessed that Chekhov would figure in it somewhere. The story would be about Chekhov as interpreted by Demetrious, Chekhov read through the eyes of her former lover. Although he had been blind to so many movements of her heart, they also shared many passions in common. Chekhov was one of them.

She spent the remainder of the ride on the Victoria line imagining how her lover would narrate the end of their relationship, once he figured out that she would never see him again. How would he describe her decision to leave him that morning in the hotel room, without even saying goodbye?

Henceforth, Teresa decided, Demetrious would become a character in her imaginary adaptation of a Chekhov play. She would become Sonya, Uncle Vanya's niece, who had wagered all her hopes on the peace that would follow after her death. Sonya was destined to become a spinster, and to manage the family the estate alone. She would set Demetrious free, free to find himself, free to find love. She would seek these same things for herself, without ever expecting to find them.

It's the search that counts, she reflected, paraphrasing Sonya, *not what you find when you reach the end of the road*. If she remained alone after searching all her life, she would at least know that, once upon a time, she had known love. She had known love with a stranger in Paris, before their relationship was brutalized by its contact with their daily lives, their everyone failings, and their egotistic blindness. For that brief rupture in the fabric of time, their souls had merged as intensely as had their bodies, while walking hand in hand along the Seine. Even if this love was destined not to last forever, surely it could make a good scene in a story that, along with several others, would comprise the story of her life.

She would never forget his deer-brown eyes, or his tender plea, just a few days into their acquaintance, that she tell him if she ever felt unloved. Of course, she never told him when she began to feel unloved. How could she have articulated such feelings when he was hurling insults at her? During those first heady days of their acquaintance his time had belonged to her and her time had belonged to him. They had shared together moments that could not be repeated, ever, by anyone. Those moments belonged to another chapter in her life, a chapter in a book that was reaching its close. The present did not erase the past.

"Goodbye, Demetrious," she whispered, kissing the air. Mind the gap, said the recorded voice on the train as they approached Trafalgar Square. She stood up to change trains.

7.

Tahdig

In the first week of the UK's nationwide Covid lockdown, the immigrant who had recently become part of her life stopped coming to visit her. Instead of meeting in her apartment, as they had done every day done before the lockdown, they met daily in Castle Park, a few minutes' walk from her home. They had first met in this park six months earlier, at a bench in the castle's shadow, so it made sense that, when they entered lockdown, their relationship resumed in this same location.

A thousand years earlier, William the Conqueror and his armies had sped through these realms, leveling everything to the ground. He built Bristol Castle to honor his conquest and secure his domain. The castle was constructed from stones that had been brought all the way from Normandy. Now the medieval castle, having been attacked during the Blitz of 1940 and reduced to ruins, stood at the center of Bristol's largest and most beautiful park, overlooking the Avon River. They sat together talking on a bench overlooking the river. It wasn't the same as being together in her home.

Every day, he brought her freshly cooked bread from his kitchen. Every loaf came in different seeds and flavors: pumpkin seeds, flax seeds, turmeric, saffron.

"What would you like me to make for you this time?" he would ask her every morning on the phone.

"Surprise me," she replied. She loved his questions even more than the food.

"You need to eat well," he whispered back into the receiver. "Your stomach needs my healthy food."

"I know," she said, "I miss your bread."

"Next time I'm going to make you special garlic bread. Do you like fresh hot garlic bread with any cheesy topping of your choice?"

She affirmed that yes, she loved garlic bread, and garlic bread with cheese was paradise itself. But it wasn't so much the food that excited her as did the thought of someone thinking carefully about her, and the food she put in her stomach.

Although the pandemic had introduced many tragedies into the world, it improved the way they spoke to each other. Anxiety and irritation yielded to a quiet calm. The fact that the world seemed to be ending and there was nothing that they could do to stop it made them yield to each other, melting in each other's arms. Their arguments faded and were replaced by a fragile equilibrium. The difficulty of seeing each other during the lockdown made them cherish every moment they spent together.

Although they came from different countries, the deepest difference between them had to do with their relationship to food. He disliked eating. Food for one's self was boring. She hated to cook, but loved eating whatever he made for her: the softness of melted Gorgonzola mixed with the scent of garlic on his homemade bread. When she ate the leftovers of a pot of rice or a cheesy golden pizza he had cooked for her late at night, her dreams that night would match the flavors he had kneaded into the dough.

The scent of the vanilla bean wafted through her imagination.

Although he loved to cook for her, he could not stand to eat with her. He hated food, and preferred to watch her take pleasure in what he crafted with his hands. It was during one of those moments, when she was greedily devouring a slice of pesto pizza—one of his many specialties—that he told her for the first time that he loved her. Her fingers pressed into the nape of his neck. They kissed. And then he pulled away, as if suddenly worried that someone might see them.

By the third week of the lockdown, she wanted more intimacy. She couldn't stand their meetings in the park anymore. She wanted to be alone with him, in her bedroom. It was time to end their isolation from each other. Time for him to return to her home.

"Can we please stop this charade?" she asked at the end of one of their meetings in the park. "Can I persuade you to visit me at home? I love your food, but I want you in my home. I'm tired of seeing you only in these public spaces."

"Sure," he said, "on one condition." He smiled. "I will cook again in your home if you prepare the ingredients for me. I want to make you crispy, crunchy, golden *tahdig*."

Although she had read about *tahdig* before, she feigned ignorance so that she could enjoy imagining him cooking it just for her.

"*Tahdig*," he explained, "is a crunchy coating that scrapes the bottom of the pot with its juicy oils and its garlicky scents. It is rice cooked to a crisp, and removed from the fire just before it burns. It has to be eaten immediately so that you can savour the crunch. It is the best food in the world, the yummiest dish in all of Iran, and it is what I miss most about my homeland."

He fell silent, consumed by memories of a distant place.

"I'll make *tahdig* for you," he said to her again. "But first I need to develop a strategy for making this Iranian dish in a foreign land. It won't taste quite the same, but I hope it will be almost as good. I want to make your *tahdig* taste just as if it had been made in Iran." He then looked at her with a knowing smile: "And you need to clean up your kitchen."

In order to clear the way for a *tahdig* feast, they agreed to take a two-week a hiatus from their regular meetings. Their hours on the phone were filled with tales of growing up eating *tahdig* in Iran. Two weeks later, she reminded him that she expected him in her home the next day.

"Of course," he said. "I don't break my promises."

And yet she wondered what would have happened had she not reminded him.

That night, alone in her kitchen and anticipating his visit, she researched hundreds of different ways to boil rice, imagining all the ways he might cook it for her. Rice with onions. Rice with curry. Rice with raisins, soaked in milk overnight. Rice with oily fish: sardines, anchovies, or salmon. Unwashed rice, called in Persian *kateh,* that sticks to your gums as you chewed it, slowly. Rice soaked overnight and rice cooked without any preparation.

She prepared for his arrival by tidying up her cluttered kitchen. Her apartment was stuffed full of knick-knacks: books, old bubble wrap, empty vials of medicine. Cans of chickpeas and kidney beans were stacked on the floor.

The kitchen merged with her living room, covering the wall closest to the entryway. A single-sized bed was pressed against the opposite wall. The room that was originally built as a bedroom she had designated as her office when she first moved in five years earlier. It stood empty and unused. She preferred to inhabit the crowded atmosphere of her kitchen/living room.

Pots and pans hung haphazardly above the stove. She scoured the ones he liked to use in his cooking until they gleamed from the steel rack like swords poised for battle. As for the rest of the pots, coated with the detritus of previous meals, she stacked them on top of each other and hid them away in the cupboard.

Soon, a pattern was established in their lives. He visited her at exactly six in the evening three days a week, and made just enough food to last her for the next couple of days.

"I'll make you something new every time I cook in your kitchen," he promised her, "until the lockdown ends. I'll make different kinds of crunchy rice coating for you until you get tired of that. Then I will make *tahdig* for you from something else, like potatoes, and even pasta."

She squeezed his hand. "I will cook for you until I disappear," he added softly.

"But you'll never disappear without warning me, right?" she asked, hoping to gain clarity about where their relationship was going.

"I was just joking," he said.

Just as he had promised, when she grew tired of rice *tahdig*, he started making for her potato *tahdig*. He gently grated her baby potatoes. Then he salted and steamed them until they formed a savory crust that melted in her mouth.

After he had exhausted the range of options for *tahdig*, he turned to desert. "I'll make you a fresh cherry drink with the syrup of cherries to go along with the potato *tahdig*," he said. "And perhaps I can learn to make *kuku sabzi* for you too. And then *mirza ghassemi*."

Along with rice, the only other mandatory ingredient from his perspective was onions. If at least two onions were not sitting on the kitchen counter when he arrived, ready for him to chop, he would enter a state of paralysis. As hard as he tried, everything he tried to cook without onions came to symbolize for him a failed experiment in expressing his love.

In order to avoid these tragic outcomes, she did her best to keep her kitchen stocked with pounds of onions and cups of rice perpetually soaking in covered bowls. To these two requirements, she added a third, which was entirely her own: garlic, every meal had to include at least three cloves of freshly-pressed garlic. She loved garlic as much for the smell, that gently tickled the hairs on her nostrils, as for its savory taste.

When they planned her meals on the phone, their imaginations ran wild, often in opposite directions. His meticulous elaboration of his cooking plans for her was a distillation of his love, he explained more than once.

As for herself, she had not cooked rice for the better part of a decade. She hardly ate cooked food at home at all before she met him. She loved watching YouTube videos about food, but actual cooking taxed her patience. He, by contrast, didn't believe in following recipes, yet loved to make food for her. One time she bought him a set of measuring cups with the idea that it would simplify his tasks in the kitchen.

"What are those?" he asked, dangling the plastic cups in the air.

"Haven't you seen them before? Measuring cups. They will make your work in the kitchen easier and more precise."

"Over my dead body," he said. He smiled and placed the cups gently in her hand.

He loved the smile that creased her face while she ate the food he had labored over, without recipes and unaided by measurements, guided only by what he called the "millennial wisdom" of generations of Iranian cooking. As for her, these moments were one of the few times in their life together when he seemed content with himself and with the world. At such moments, it seemed that they were united: one body, one flesh, one heart, one soul.

Finally, after three months of him cooking tahdig covertly in her kitchen, the end of lockdown was announced. Individuals who belonged to separate households were permitted to visit each other again, though they were advised to wear masks everywhere they went. Now, finally, he could cook for her publicly, without concealing his entrances and exits from the world.

On the morning of his first visit after the relaxing of government restrictions, she set out the ingredients on the kitchen counter. She had dreamed the night before of the food he would make for her. In the end, she decided on one of his favorites: *polo Istanbuli*, rice Istanbul style, with green beans, red onions, and a thick garlicky tomato puree that turned the pearly white rice the color of a crimson sunset. She dreamed of the *tahdig* that would emerge from this bloody concoction.

Just as he had always done, his insisted that the rice be freshly soaked the night before. Before the lockdown, she had often cheated and only started soaking the rice a few hours before his arrival. She always kept such lapses secret from him. This morning, however, she followed his instructions as if they were a religious dictum. Then she sat down on her bed, her coffee mug filled to the brim, and awaited his arrival.

A week after the lockdown had come to an end, he arrived looking downcast. She knew better than to ask what was wrong. Too often in the past, such questions had steered their conversation in dark directions that neither of them wanted it to go. She sat down on her unmade bed, the sheets piled on top each other, and watched him get to work.

"What would you like for dinner?" he asked.

She smiled and glanced at a bowl of washed rice. "I think you already know without my asking."

"*Tahdig*?" he said.

She nodded. It was like they had been exchanging words of love.

He took off his shirt, and flexed his muscles, as if he were preparing to lift weights. He picked up the bowl with the soaked rice and started washing it vigorously. He drained the water and washed the grains again. Then he did it a third time, to remove all the starch.

"Does it need to be washed so many times?" she asked.

"Yes," he said. "The *tahdig* has to shine."

He chopped the garlic and onions and sautéed them together in a thick layer of extra virgin olive oil. Then he sprinkled the turmeric powder she kept on the countertop, just for him.

"Don't onions make you cry?" she asked, the brims of her eyelids growing itchy with tears.

"A little bit," he said, "but it doesn't matter. It's a price I'm willing to pay to cook for the one I love."

It seemed strange to her that anyone could express their love in the way he did, by cooking. She almost couldn't believe it was love, until she looked at him, at his back hunched over the saucepan, and at his hands stirring vigorously.

As he cooked, she dwelled on how the lockdown had been punctured by so much suffering. The death toll was too high to count. She wanted to tell him about a scene she had witnessed a month after their forced separation: a woman was overtaken by coughing in the grocery store, and the ambulance arrived to take her away.

But she knew better than to interrupt his cooking. She watched him silently, stirring the onions as they caramelized, then pouring the onion mix, along with the golden turmeric and savory garlic, into the rice with the green beans and the tomato puree.

"Will you eat with me?" she asked, knowing the answer in advance.

"I already ate," he said. "I'm making this for *you.* Cooking is an expression of my love. A lover should not eat the food made with his own hands."

The sun shot through the window and cast its rays on his muscular back, bent over the stove, stirring the sauce that was to accompany the *tahdig.* She reflected on how little she understood about his love. *Won't we regret someday leaving so much unsaid?* she wondered. *What will happen we stop speaking the truth to each other?*

What will we do then? All that she knew for certain was that she loved him. She wanted to build her life with him. He did not seem to know what he wanted from life, other than to cook *tahdig* for her.

Savoring every bite, she thought of how pampered she had been by his cooking throughout the lockdown: crunchy, yet not too hard on the teeth, flavored with garlic, salt, and turmeric along the edges. He could tell it was a success, and was proud of being able to give her pleasure in this way, by making rice that melted in her mouth.

She wanted to ask the questions that had been tormenting her for months—what were his plans and intentions, what was the future of their relationship, what was his future on this earth—but she knew he preferred to watch her eat. She could not bear to spoil the gentle smile on his face. The peace he had attained by making her *tahdig* was as fragile as a rainbow after a drought, and as beautiful when refracted through the prism of his eyes. So she let the questions subside. Surely there would be another occasion to ask them.

The next day, he made her potato *tahdig*. Then he decided to make the most of the sunny season and bought her a pint of cherries for *albalu polo*, cherry rice. He used the leftover syrup from the cherries to make her an icy sorbet that captured all the colors of the setting sun. She sipped the icy slush slowly, as if it were nectar from heaven.

Every morning, she set out vegetables for him to chop and mix with the rice: carrots, bell peppers, parsnips, sometimes also raisins. He preferred to stick to traditional Iranian cuisine, but sometimes she convinced him to take a risk.

"It's time to try something different," she said. "In cooking as well as life."

He smiled, but ignored her last remark.

"We can't access all those fruits and vegetables you get in Iran," she said. "We have to make do with genetically modified crops, especially after lockdown. But I love everything you make for me, simply because it is made by you."

It was always she who did the talking, and he did the cooking.

Every time he cooked, he revealed to her a new dimension of his home country. They couldn't visit Iran together under the current political system, so they had to travel in their imaginations, with the help of Iranian flavors and scents.

He always refused her invitation to eat with him.

He didn't like talking about difficult things.

The precarious moments that they shared together were a kind of paradise on earth.

These routines persisted for several more months. Peace and calm dominated every meeting, as did good food, good drink, and good eating.

The pandemic gradually faded from the headlines. People continued to die in large numbers, especially in faraway places, but their deaths ceased to be breaking news.

He washed his hands vigorously every time he crossed her threshold, and took his temperature every morning, fearful not for himself, but of infecting her. As for himself, he welcomed the sickness. It would be an easy solution to his problems, a way out of his precarity, he explained on one particularly gloomy day.

Then one day, he was late. She waited and waited for his knock on the door. Hours passed, but he never came. No one picked up when she dialled his phone number. She called the few acquaintances of his that she knew: the neighbor for whom he baked bread from time to time, the Palestinian grocer who sold fresh parsley across the street from his apartment block. No one knew where he was.

She never found out what happened to him, whether he had died, or simply vanished from the world, as he had many times threatened to do. At first, she was shocked: what kind of lover would simply disappear from the life of the woman with whom he had passed so many cherished days? What kind of love was that? Perhaps he had never really cared about her at all.

Then she remembered what he had said to her one night, not long before he disappeared. "If you never see me again," he said, "just remember that the situation was beyond my control. Unlike you, I am not in control of my own destiny."

He often talked like that, full of cryptic innuendos that she couldn't grasp. She didn't pay much attention to his words at the time. She knew that his application for a renewal of his visa was pending, and the result was uncertain. But ultimately, she had faith in the British system. Surely they would not deport a deserving migrant like himself, especially during a pandemic? There were so many ways in which he could work for the betterment of his host country, not least by enriching British cuisine with his *tahdig*.

No matter how desperately hard she tried, she never learned to cook *tahdig*, or any of his other specialties, in the way he had done for her. Even when she used exactly the same ingredients as he had used, purchased them from the same Palestinian grocer, and chopped the onions just as he had done, caramelizing them at the same temperature and for the same amount of time, the food didn't taste the same. It wasn't made with love. She remembered his words to her: *we should never eat the food that we have prepared for ourselves, only the food that others made for us, with love.* She went back to eating processed foods.

8.

Like a Cavafy Poem

Their coming together was like a Cavafy poem. When they lay in each other's arms, time compressed into space, and space condensed into time. Every anger, every resentment wrapped them more deeply into the folds of each other's affections, like an old sweater that feels better on the skin than a new shirt even when its rough touch wounds. When they were together, obstacles standing in the way of their union suddenly lifted. The walls dividing them came tumbling down.

Lovemaking was a path to creation. Their words became flesh, so that something on this earth—not everything, just the body of language, the crusts of consciousness—would outlive them both.

"I don't want to die," she said to him once. They were walking along the canals of Amsterdam as afternoon edged into evening. The sun creased the horizon crimson while cumulus clouds mounted in the sky. "I want to live forever, with you holding my hands."

He didn't speak. There was nothing to be said. They were mere creatures inside a Cavafy poem, the one where the body remembers how much it was loved, and how it gave itself to that love, as if there were no turning back, and the only movement was forward, into the abyss. All words could do was freeze their union in time, giving it the appearance of a coherence it lacked. Their love was too perfect for their fleeting world, too immaculate for language.

Sometimes they spoke to each other eloquently, almost as if in verse. Sometimes they didn't speak at all. Instead, they traced the outlines of each other's faces in the palms of their hands. Sometimes they hid naked beneath the sheets, like children hiding from their parents. Sometimes they read together, softly whispering to each other the words that glowed on the page. Every syllable seemed to be about them, in one way or another.

They shared together bright, sharp slices of time, flashes of lightning on the water: kissing for the first time on the Danube, crossing the bridges of the Thames, holding hands while overlooking the Seine. Notre Dame hovered above them, its spires charred.

There was love between them, and there was something else too: a meeting of minds, a merging of intellects, an unveiling of each other's bodies, an uttering of each other's words. And that uttering—that savouring of the other's being—entered into their souls. The intimacy spilled onto the page, binding their togetherness and bridging its absence, causing them to feel with every act of lovemaking that they were giving something back to the universe. They created, alone and together, things that would never have been born had they not crossed paths. Lightning flashed on the water when they stared at it together.

When they were apart, she hardened her heart against him. Not because she did not love him, but because her love existed outside of her control. She could not bear the open wounds that festered within her, the stigmata of her helplessness. She was tormented by his inability to soothe her wounds, to caress her and to heal them with the balm of his affection when she needed him most.

There were times too when he was absent even when he was present, when her words failed to penetrate his soul. Having spent all his life fighting battles in faraway countries, he could not see her battle scars. Her struggles seemed miniscule compared to his. He admired her too much.

Sometimes he treated her like an idol rather than a lover, so it seemed to her. *Idolatry is always false*, she told him many times, but it made no difference. The loneliness of being alone, she concluded, was easier than the loneliness that overcame her after she sought comfort and kinship from him and failed to find it.

Every time they shared their souls, the stars aligned, cursing them to an eternity of unsaid goodbyes.

"I don't want to die," she said again, two years into their relationship.

This time, the words had a meaning different from when she had uttered them by the canal in Amsterdam, even though the words had been the same. She had contracted cancer, and it was spreading within her faster than she cared to know. The doctors told her she had less than a year to live.

Yet still, he could not be with her when she wanted him to, could not decipher her battle scars, could not recognize her as a suffering creature. He loved her too much and in the wrong way, as if she were a character in his favorite book, or an actress in his favorite play. For him, she was a figment—beloved yet forever fictional—of his fecund imagination, the one that gave birth while making love.

In death, they came together again, and it was like a Cavafy poem.

9.

Goodbye, Home

The enemy is the embodiment of your own question.

—Theodor Däubler

I. Oakland, 2014

In 1930, five years after giving up hope of an academic career, Walter Benjamin sent a book to legal theorist Carl Schmitt, who would soon become a leading jurist for the Third Reich. Benjamin had hoped that the book would earn him a professorship at the University of Frankfurt, but instead it marked the end of his academic ambitions. The letter was succinct:

Esteemed Professor Schmitt,

I have derived from your later works…a confirmation of my modes of research in the philosophy of art from yours in the philosophy of the state.

It was signed:

With my expression of special admiration,

> *Yours very humbly,*
> *Walter Benjamin*

Jeremiah came across this letter in the open stacks of UC Berkeley's Gardner Library in the summer of 2015. It was his last year at the university. He had been pursuing a BA degree with a double major in German and Rhetoric.

A few weeks after coming across the letter, he left the university, just a few credits short of a degree. He could not endure any more sessions of the final required class for his major. Instead of using class time to discuss the Musil's novel *The Man without Qualities* and Döblin's *Alexanderplatz*, the professor spent his lectures explaining why the world had failed to recognize his brilliance. So Jeremiah quit, uncertain of his prospects, and unable to say what the future held in store. All he knew was that he could no longer continue as a student. If Walter Benjamin couldn't make it as an academic, he decided, university life was not for him either. He returned to his library books and found a job as a barista in the cafe across the street from his apartment in downtown Oakland. He started working the nightshift, 8pm to 2am, Monday to Friday, every night.

Jeremiah spent his weekends reading Edward Said, James Baldwin, Jean Genet, and his longest-standing passion, Walter Benjamin. Each man's picture was pasted to his refrigerator. He paused to gaze at them every time he brewed coffee. He also spent this time reconnecting with Judaism, a religion he had avoided thinking about ever since his mother's death three years earlier. She had been an Orthodox Jew, and a first-generation immigrant, born to parents from the Pale of Settlement. They had reached Ellis Island in 1912. She had been determined to raise her son in the Orthodox tradition.

Every time he called her or visited her in her rent-controlled Lower East Side apartment, she asked:

"When will you find a nice Jewish girl to marry?"

He had got so fed up with this question that he stopped calling her. On the day she died, he told himself that his Judaism was forever buried beneath the earth, in her grave.

Now, freed from both his mother and the pressures of coursework, Jeremiah began reading avidly in the history of Judaism. He rediscovered old texts that he had always meant to read but never had: Maimonides, Ibn Ezra, Gershom Scholem, Levinas. As he immersed himself in radical Jewish thought from Marx to Emma Goldman, Judaism came to seem like a different kind of religion. It was not a religion at all, he realized. It was more like a philosophy of life. He had never imagined Judaism like this in his childhood. He read the writings of Bernard Lazare, the anarchist-turned-Zionist following the Dreyfus affair. And then Emma Goldman, Alexander Berkman, and the anarchists in their circle, nearly all of whom were Jewish. Finally, he turned to Jewish messianism, from Sabbatai Zevi to Gershom Scholem.

At long last he arrived at Benjamin. He lingered on Benjamin for many weeks, often reading the same sentences twice. He stopped reading when he encountered Benjamin's correspondence with Scholem, teaching him Hebrew and seeking to persuade him to immigrate to Palestine. He did not feel up to grappling with Benjamin's take on Zionism. What if he accepted Israel as a legitimate state, and the expulsion of Palestinians to make that state possible? That would open up a whole new set of problems, which he had no strategy for dealing with. Not yet. If he had learned one thing from his professors at Berkeley, it was that Israel's existence was an affront to human rights and a threat to international peace.

All this time, he avoided reading Schmitt, although the German theorist loomed everywhere on his horizon: in his reading about Walter Benjamin, about the Third Reich, and in critiques of liberalism. Jeremiah refused to categorize himself politically, but he hated liberalism. Everywhere he turned, Schmitt's ideas resonated with his intuitions about the violence of politics and its religious dimensions. Yet he was not ready to encounter Schmitt himself. He did not feel prepared to deal with the ethical complexities of engaging with a Nazi just yet, even one admired by Benjamin. First, he had to come to terms with the Israeli occupation. Then—and only then—could he face Schmitt's Nazi legacy.

For the remainder of that year, most of Jeremiah's conversations were limited to strangers on the street and in stores. They consisted of one-liners: *Hello, Goodbye, Thank You.* Only one activity broke through this routine of silence with the outside world: sex.

During the initial phase of his immersion in reading, he managed to go without sex for weeks and then months at a time. But when he passed the six-month mark without sex, masturbation could no longer satisfy him. He started to long for the feeling of another's flesh against his own. So he took to visiting a bar every Sunday night to pick up women. He avoided Saturday nights, when competition was greatest, and he stood the least chance of triumphing over his rivals. Every woman to whom he was attracted on those nights had paired up with someone by around 9pm. His chances were better on Sundays. Attractive women lingered alone until around 11pm. He developed a routine of reaching the bar by 10:30 and walked in nonchalantly, glancing straight ahead. He would then head directly for the pool table, from which he watched women file into the bar from an angle that hid his face while providing a panoramic vista of every body in his field of vision.

When he found a woman he wanted to sleep with, he would buy her two drinks and then invite her home. They would typically have sex within a few minutes of her arrival. At first, these predictable encounters were appealing, but after two months they became tedious. It always ended the same way: first, excitement, followed by loss, then alienation, then a feeling akin to hatred.

He could not explain the intensity of his repulsion for the woman by his side. It became increasingly difficult to have an erection, and his penis would grow flaccid in the middle of the sex. If the woman he was with was menstruating, that gave him an alibi for his failure to get an erection: he would explain to her that Jewish law forbids sex with a menstruating woman. But most of the women he brought home were not bleeding.

Finally, after one particularly trying night, when, after a half hour of effort, he could not manage to penetrate the girl he had brought home, he wondered aloud whether getting an erection might not be easier with a man.

"Sounds like you need to experiment a bit," said the girl he had failed to penetrate as she alternated between stroking his hair and massaging his body. They were sitting on opposite ends of the bed, in the aftermath of his failed attempt at sex. She was a perfect simulacrum of stereotypical female beauty, with a narrow figure and long blonde hair.

The more he looked at her, the more preoccupied he became by the idea of touching—and being touched by—a man. When he finally managed to enter her that night, he imagined being penetrated by a man. He woke up early in the morning to the discovery that he had had a wet dream during the night.

Life proceeded according to this routine for three years. The only major change was that he started going to gay bars and bringing men home instead of women. He continued to nourish himself on books. After three years of limbo in between dropping out of university and working as a barista at the café across the street, he decided it was time for a change. Of routine, as well as location. So, when the new year arrived, he booked a one-way ticket to a city he had never visited before, but which had long been the subject of his dreams.

"Goodbye, home," he said quietly to himself as he stepped onto the ramp that connected to the plane in San Francisco International Airport that would take him across the Atlantic. He felt that he was saying goodbye, not just to Oakland and to Berkeley, but to his childhood home in New York City as well. He was saying goodbye to his mother, to his past, and to the country of his birth.

II. **London, 2017**

Getting a job in London—again as a barista, this time with three years of experience—was easy. Finding a place to live was another matter. He was determined to reside in the city centre but had not been prepared for the cost of rent. £1000 per month was the cheapest he could find for a room in King's Cross that didn't even include a private bathroom. A new word entered his vocabulary: *bedsit*, a term used to describe a space so small that it couldn't fit an entire bed, so the bed had to be hoisted up during the day and transformed into a sofa. He learned that even people living in such primitive and cramped conditions were expected to pay council tax, which raised the cost of living by twenty percent.

Financially, London was a struggle. Yet, he loved his newly adopted city. He adored the juxtapositions of old and new: ancient Roman ruins, the medieval Tower of London, early modern operating theatres, Big Ben, and skyscrapers like The Shard. He loved the banners, launched by London's mayor Sadiq Khan, proclaiming: ALL ARE WELCOME HERE in the languages of the world. He rejoiced every night as he walked home from Euston Station to King's Cross following a long day of brewing coffee and tea at Ozone Roasters. Every new day helped him to discover a new side of himself. Jeremiah started to consider what it would be like to live in London for the rest of his life. Every night he roamed London's streets the more it felt like home. All he was missing was a companion. He didn't so much long for a specific person as he longed for a body to touch and be touched by.

One cold December afternoon, a year following his move to London, Jeremiah sat in a café near Victoria Station, watching commuters on their way home after work. While he waited, he recollected his college days, four years earlier. He had read many books since then, had seen more of the world, and had grown used to sex with men, but otherwise he remained the same. Schmitt continued to intimidate him. He reflected on how his reading preferences during his college years—especially the Frankfurt School and Jewish mysticism—shaped him, long after he had relocated to London.

Jeremiah had been recognized as a talented barista for his deep knowledge of coffee beans and for his mastery of the roasting process. He attributed his coffee roasting skills to his extensive reading in the university library, as well as to his immersion in books after he left the university. During the past month, he had returned to his old preoccupation with the correspondence between Benjamin and Schmitt.

Even though Benjamin and Schmitt never met, they had a special connection, as Benjamin's letter attested, and Schmitt's later writings, published after Benjamin's death, proved. Jeremiah recollected a line that Schmitt loved to quote, from his German poet friend, Theodor Däubler: *Der Feind ist unsere eigene Frage als Gestalt. The enemy is the embodiment of your own question.* Schmitt had served the same Nazi regime that had led Benjamin to end his life.

Jeremiah wondered: Were they friends or enemies? Or both? And what did Benjamin's admiration for Schmitt mean for his obsession with Israel/Palestine, a conflict that was all about enmity and enduring hatreds? Could Schmitt's friend/enemy distinction help him craft a politics for Jewish engagement with Israel, the pariah state and betrayer of everything that was good in Judaism? Or would obsessing over it simply entrench ancient antagonisms and increase his hostility towards his political antagonists?

In contrast to the earlier phase in his life when he posed these questions back in Oakland, Jeremiah finally felt up to the challenge posed by Schmitt. Yet he knew he could not handle Schmitt alone. In search of answers, Jeremiah contacted one of London's leading lawyers: Stefan Grimes QC, who had his offices in Bedford Chambers, LLC. Born in Berlin, Stefan move to the UK to attend Oxford and never returned to Germany. Although he had a PhD from the London School of Economics in legal theory, Stefan had made a career for himself outside academia. He had argued cases at the International Court of Justice, the International Criminal Court in The Hague, and the European Court of Human Rights in Strasbourg.

Grimes's books dealt with the Austrian jurist Hans Kelsen, the role of international law in the creation of the state of Israel, and, most importantly for Jeremiah, Schmitt's political theology. Although the Schmitt book was Grimes' magnum opus, his book on Israel had received wider recognition. Due to its presentation of the creation of Israel as the first triumph of international law in the post-World War II era, it had been awarded the Israel Prize. Reviewers in *The Times of Israel* and *The Algeimeiner* praised the book as a "tour de force." They singled out for praise the argument that the expansion of settlements across the Green Line were consistent with international law. A special event at the Israeli embassy was convened in honor of the book's publication. Yet, in Jeremiah's opinion, it was in the Schmitt book, and not in his morally questionable defences of the Israeli state, that Grimes' brilliance shone. Amazingly, he had authored these tomes while maintaining a full-time practice in international law.

Jeremiah was drawn to men like Stefan, whose intellect was closely linked to their politics, and whose works shaped public debate. He was also drawn to the twinkle in Stefan's eyes that peered at him from every photograph of him posted online, and every YouTube clip that he diligently watched, multiple times. So he decided to risk an email, to explain his interest in his book and in Schmitt, and to ask if they could meet. "I want to use Schmitt," he explained, "to resolve the conflict in Palestine." He had prepared himself for rejection, or non-response. Yet the exchange led Grimes to suggest that they meet. And that's how he ended up in Ozone cafe across from Victoria Station on Friday afternoon in the midst of London's rush hour, waiting for the man whose words excited his soul and whose eyes—as seen on his website profile—made him breathe faster than normal.

While he was immersed in reflecting on what he might say to Stefan, a tall man walked up to him and extended his hand. He was impeccably dressed, in a black suit and a silk red tie that made him look as if he had just emerged from a courtroom. Jeremiah caught the scent of aftershave from his clean-shaven chin.

"You must be Jeremiah," he said with a bright smile.

"And you must be Stefan," Jeremiah said, distracted by the scent of the aftershave. "Thanks for agreeing to meet. Please sit." Jeremiah gestured towards the seat across from him. "I ordered coffee for us both. I hope that's ok."

Stefan sat down. They stared at each other for some time. The emails they had exchanged prior to meeting had been full of philosophical musings, propelled by endless questions and the impossibility of answering them all. So many imponderables had been raised as they probed each other's intellects. And yet so much remained unknown, including the basics: where they were born and raised, how many siblings they had, what their parents had done for a living, what they liked to eat, their favorite music.

After minutes of quiet staring, it began to feel awkward for them both. Yet it was exciting to see each other finally in the flesh after countless virtual exchanges.

Finally, Jeremiah broke the silence: "I love your book."

"My book?" Stefan said in confusion, as if he had temporarily forgotten that the meaning of the word.

"Your book. I love all your books of course. But I mean the last one, on Schmitt."

Stefan smiled. "You made that clear over email. I'm glad you liked it. No one else did."

This was followed by a long pause. "Can I ask you a personal question?" Stefan asked at last.

Jeremiah nodded eagerly. Any sign of interest in him from Stefan was more than welcome.

"Why are you obsessed with Israel? Are you Jewish?"

There was only one answer to that question. He was a Jew who opposed the policies of the state of Israel. Indeed, he opposed Israel itself, and the idea of a Jewish state. He was a Jew who rejected Zionism, and supported Palestinian human rights. Judaism was the religion into which he was born. Marxism was the religion had chosen for himself, as filtered through Adorno, Horkheimer, and other members of the Frankfurt School. Walter Benjamin was the image of the intellectual he wanted to become. Along with being a cultural Marxist, he also supported a cultural boycott of Israel, but he hesitated to share that with Stefan just yet. He decided to answer the second part of the question while ignoring the first.

"I'm a Jewish Marxist," Walter said with a smile. "What about you?"

"Me?" Stefan smiled back. "I suppose you could call me an atheist. I'm definitely not a Jew."

"Ok, but that doesn't tell me much about your background. How do you identify? What culture do you come from?"

Stefan flashed a mischievous smile. "Is that why you asked to meet me? So you could pinpoint my identity? Categorize me? Erase my individuality? I am not a category." he paused and, when he got no response, continued, "Why did you ask to meet, if I may ask?"

Jeremiah paused. In fact, he had not asked to meet. A meeting had been Grimes' suggestion. He surveyed the café. Victoria Station was visible in the distance. Workers rushed towards the Tube station full of dreams for the weekend. Finally, he summoned the courage to stare back at his interlocutor.

"I want you to teach me to read Schmitt," he said slowly. "I've read him before, through the eyes of Benjamin, but I was never able to understand him like you do. Like a lawyer. When I read your book, I start thinking about Schmitt differently. I began to think that if Schmitt were alive he could help me understand power. And if I understand power, then I can create peace. I want you to teach me about the friend/enemy distinction as described by Schmitt."

Stefan looked at him quizzically, "How can such arcane political concepts help you bring about peace?"

Jeremiah smiled, knowing that what he was about to say would sound absurd to a lawyer's ears. "Understanding power will help me grasp the political logic of the Israeli state. Schmitt will help me resolve the conflict between Israel and Palestine." He suddenly realized that he was sounding like a megalomaniac. Tempering his words, he added: "I want to bring justice to Palestinians."

"Only to Palestinians?" Stefan asked. "What about Israelis?"

"Justice for Palestinians means justice for Israelis," Jeremiah said.

They stared at each other without fear. This new intimacy aroused Jeremiah's desire, and the crossing of boundaries seemed to mark a new frontier. He was no longer afraid to stare at this man who so dazzled him. This was clearly not the conversation that Stefan had been expecting. Yet Jeremiah was not surprised. Stefan's politics had long been clear to Jeremiah from his monthly columns in *The Daily Telegraph* and *The Spectator*. Jeremiah knew that they diverged on most matters related to Israel, but it was too early in their relationship to enter that terrain. Finally, Stefan asked after a long silence: "What makes you think I can teach you to read Schmitt? Didn't they teach you anything at Berkeley?"

"No," Jeremiah said flatly. "At Berkeley they taught us to read authors historically and contextually, to measure influence, and to imitate precedents. They taught us to pose as leftists. They didn't teach us to think for ourselves or to change the world."

Stefan laughed. "You think I can teach such things to you?"

"Well, you've been making a difference in court for decades," Jeremiah said. "And with great success."

Another long pause. Amid the hustle and bustle outside, the blue sky was streaked with gold, burnished by the setting sun. It was only five in the afternoon, but the scintillating sky made it feel like work was a distant horizon and the day was done. "Ok, so let's say I teach you how to read Schmitt. What do I get in return?"

Jeremiah paused as he tried to imagine suitable remuneration. "You get my eternal gratitude," he finally said. "You also get to play a role in bringing peace to the Middle East."

They stared at each other for nearly a minute in silence as the crowd bustled past. Normally, Jeremiah would have felt awkward staring and being stared at by someone he'd only just met, but this was different. He and Stefan had engaged each other's intellects by email for weeks prior to their meeting. Jeremiah had strategically refrained from mentioning Israel, but their exchanges had touched on intensely political subjects: migration, Brexit, Corbyn. Every argument they had brought them closer together.

Jeremiah had been aware from Grimes' other writings of their sharp differences when it came to the legitimacy of the Jewish state and its actions in the Occupied Territories. Grimes, in true Schmittian spirit, sided with the sovereign power. "The sovereign," he insisted in op-ed after op-ed and most extensively in his book, is "he who decides on the exception." Grimes believed in the sovereign's absolute authority and understood it to be intrinsic to the legitimacy of the modern state. In his capacity as legal consultant to Parliament's Foreign Affairs Committee, Grimes had argued that the UK should withhold recognition of Palestine and direct its diplomatic efforts to securing Israel's security. Israel, he explained, was the only democracy in the Middle East, and the only government that could guarantee regional peace.

For Grimes, Israel was an abstraction, a testing ground for his legal theories, not a place inhabited by people he loved. Israel was an abstraction for Jeremiah too, in the opposite sense that it was a place he detested. What they shared was a sense of Israel and Palestine as symbols, signs with which their destinies were intertwined.

Jeremiah reflected on how his mortality seemed to hinge on the hope that he would see a Palestinian state and a free Palestine within his lifetime. And what if he did not? What if he died in the middle of an Israeli genocide of Palestine? What if the genocide brought about the end of the world?

Jeremiah's daydream was interrupted by Stefan's hand. "It's a deal," he said, lightly grazing his palm. Stefan rose to leave. "How are you getting home?" he asked.

They were both taking the Victoria Line, although in opposite directions. They walked together to the station.

"When can I see you again?" Jeremiah asked him at the station, slightly surprised by his boldness.

"How about next week?"

Jeremiah nodded assent.

"Same time, same place," Stefan suggested. "Don't forget to bring Schmitt." He touched him lightly on the shoulder and hurried to catch the train.

Jeremiah spent the next week preparing for their meeting that Friday. He started with Schmitt's textbook on constitutional theory, *Verfassungslehre,* and reread Schmitt's early works, including *Political Theology* and *The Concept of the Political.* He welcomed the opportunity to immerse himself in the work of a thinker who had been so important to his hero Walter Benjamin. And yet, the pleasure he took in reading Schmitt was inseparable from his excitement at doing so through the eyes of Stefan Grimes, one of the UK's most distinguished lawyers, whose deep green eyes had a way of making him feel flustered.

Jeremiah arrived an hour earlier to their scheduled meeting. He wanted to make sure he had time to pick a good table, away from the crowd, to lay out his Schmitt books in chronological order, to organize his paper and pencils neatly in a row, and to stock up on drinks.

He chose a table in the corner and ordered cappuccinos for them both, along with two tall glasses of lemonade. Stefan arrived exactly when the clock hanging over the entrance chimed five. He was as impeccably groomed as before, in a neatly ironed suit with a crimson silk tie. Jeremiah rose to greet him. The greeting became a handclasp that became a hug.

Stefan sat down and asked: "What have you been up to?"

"Reading Schmitt," Jeremiah responded, "just like you told me to."

Jeremiah reached into his backpack and pulled out a purple notebook. Frayed along the edges, the notebook was folded along the middle. It had his name written on it in a hasty script: Jeremiah Cohen. He handed it over to Stefan, who flipped through it casually, pausing over certain pages to scrutinize the script.

"I see you've been busy," he said after he reached the middle of the notebook. "Did you compile all those notes since we met last week?"

"Yes, I did." Jeremiah smiled. He felt unaccountably proud of himself, as if he were still in primary school and Stefan was his teacher. "Can you read my handwriting?"

"Not really." Stefan smiled. "We'll work on that later. For now, I want you to focus on your note-taking methods. You need to be systematic, not haphazard like this. Create a column on one side for the pages you quote from, then summarize the quotations. Then explain to which principle of jurisprudence this particular citation from Schmitt corresponds. Draw on the classic common law commentaries, for example Blackstone's."

They spent the rest of the meeting discussing recent

developments within Israel. Settlement expansion was proceeding apace. The United States had declared Jerusalem as Israel's capital. Congress was poised to pass a law criminalising the cultural boycott of Israel, and Germany had just done so. At the same time, Netanyahu would not be in power forever. This last point was the only one on which they both agreed.

As for the others, Stefan said, "It's about time the world recognized that Israel is here to stay. About time to recognize Israel's right to exist."

"To exist at what cost?" Jeremiah asked. "The destruction and dispossession of the Palestinian people."

Stefan grinned and refused to answer.

Jeremiah took Stefan's advice to heart. He arrived to their next meeting, at the same Ozone café in Victoria Station, on a Friday in the late afternoon as commuters hurried home, with another notebook, also perforated and frayed at the edges. This time the passages were organized into columns and rows streamlined, just as Stefan had requested. He had also taken pains to write more legibly.

"Is it better this time?" Jeremiah asked after Stefan flipped through the notebook for several minutes straight.

"Yes, better," Stefan said, "but still not good enough."

Jeremiah was disappointed. "How can I make my notes good enough for you?" he asked.

Stefan persisted in his customary stare. After taking in Jeremiah's ruby red, questioning lips for several seconds, he said: "It's not me you have to please! It's Schmitt, the toughest critic I know."

Jeremiah smiled. He was both frustrated and elated. He realized he might never satisfy Stefan but felt compelled to try. Was he prepared to continue in this way forever? They sat in silence for several minutes, waiting for the other to speak.

Eventually, Jeremiah realized that it wasn't only the desire to master Schmitt that drew him to Stefan. Stefan himself was the main attraction. He wanted to know more about the man behind the crisp image, outside the courtroom, away from the office. What was Stefan like when there was no one he had to impress?

"Can I ask you a personal question?" Jeremiah said slowly, deliberately reproducing the tone Stefan had used when asking whether he was Jewish during their first meeting.

"Of course!" Stefan said. His smile suggested that he caught the innuendo.

"Would you ever consider travelling outside the UK?" Jeremiah asked slowly.

"Of course!" Stefan said, bemused. "I practically live outside the UK, at The Hague and in Strasbourg."

"What about with me?" Jeremiah asked, even slower than before. He was shocked by his own words, and unsure of what he wanted or why he uttered them.

For once, Stefan seemed caught off guard. "What do you mean?" he asked.

"To Israel," Jeremiah said. The words seemed to suggest themselves spontaneously. "I mean Palestine. I mean both—."

Stefan looked at him quizzically. "What would we do?"

"We'll visit the refugee camps. We'll see Jerusalem. We'll pass through checkpoints. I'll show you a world you've never seen before. I'll show you things you've never even heard of, which the media has kept concealed. And just to make you happy, we'll visit the settlements."

Stefan smiled. "Why would that make me happy?"

"You know you've always dreamt of becoming a settler!" Jeremiah joked.

Stefan raised his eyebrows. "Maybe you know me better than I know myself." Stefan stared at Jeremiah with his customary intensity. Jeremiah felt as if he were drilling a hole into his forehead with his gaze. "When do you want to go?" he asked at last.

"The first week in January."

III. **Ben Gurion Airport, 2018**

They met at Heathrow, at six on a Sunday morning in January, to board a direct flight to Ben Gurion airport on the outskirts of Tel Aviv, the only international airport in all of Israel and Palestine. During a brief window of time, from 1998 to 2000, Yasser Arafat International Airport had flown cargo internationally into Egypt, but that time was long past. Now, Israel controlled all border crossings into Palestine, and Gaza was under siege.

Jeremiah packed light, as he always did for long trips, with all his belongings stuffed into the same backpack he had used at Berkeley. When they were seated together in the very last row of the plane, He pulled out a large book with arches on the cover and showed it to Stefan.

"Now it's my turn to teaching you something," he said. "You've taught me so much about Schmitt. I want to return the favour by teaching you about Walter Benjamin."

They passed the entire flight reading from Benjamin's *Arcades Project*. The work's fragmentary structure made it perfect for sharing together. Jeremiah would read a line, and then Stefan would venture an interpretation, following which Jeremiah would correct him. Although Schmitt had first brought them into contact, Jeremiah felt that it was Benjamin who made them intimate with each other.

As they read of Benjamin's wanderings through the Paris arcades, Jeremiah listed the arcades of other cities he dreamed of visiting: Brussels, Milan, Istanbul, Bath, St. Petersburg, Moscow, Aleppo.

"I've been to all of these cities," Stefan said.

"I hope you'll be willing to visit them again," Jeremiah said. After a pause he added: "with me," and let the words hang silently in the air.

As soon as they stepped off the plane, they faced a cluster of five guards armed with machine guns. Israelis were allowed to pass into their own customs area, but foreigners had to remain behind. One of the guards address the crowd: "Your passport, please."

Among the crowd of foreigners, Stefan was the first to hand over his passport. He chose. To provide his German one. The guard barely glanced at it before handing it back to Stefan.

"Willkommen in Israel!" He was wearing army fatigues just like the IDF soldiers Jeremiah had seen in movies depicting the Israeli occupation.

Jeremiah handed over his US passport to another guard, who refused to meet his gaze. The guard flipped slowly through its many pages, scrutinizing each visa and holding every page up to the light. The countries Jeremiah had visited were hardly exotic—Germany, the Netherlands, Italy—yet the guard was suspicious.

"Why did you come to Israel?" the guard finally asked.

"To make peace," Jeremiah said. Not getting a response to these words, he added even more provocatively: "To end the occupation."

Stefan stood nearby, watching the exchange silently and running his fingers through his hair. In place of his normally composed demeanour, anxiety cast a pall over his face.

"Please step aside," the guard said when he had finished flipping through the pages of Jeremiah's passport. Stefan stepped backward to join them but another guard restrained him.

Jeremiah was ushered into a dilapidated waiting room, full of refugees from Eritrea and Sudan. They were part of a group that had crossed over into Israel from Egypt when the fence in the Sinai Peninsula was unguarded. Only the babies seemed unafraid. The air was thick with smoke and the seats shimmered with sweat.

Jeremiah had read about the increasing number of deportations of new arrivals to Israel in news reports by the alternative press, in places such as *Mondoweiss*, *Electronic Intifada*, and *972+*. Human Rights Watch had been reporting on such incidents regularly, while the European Union looked the other way, and the US reiterated Israel's right to self-defence. Reading these reports, Jeremiah had always imagined someone else being the target, but never himself. How could he, a Jew, be banned from entering Israel? What would his mother say?

His mother, who had raised him as Jewish, had forced him to attend a Hebrew school every weekend again his will, from whom he had learnt to read the Torah and Sholem Aleichem? She had encouraged him to make *aliyah* ever since he graduated from high school, and every time he called her from Oakland. Back then he had ignored her request. Now he had hoped to fulfil his dead mother's dream, only to learn that he might be forbidden from entering Israel forever. He wondered whether his mother was watching him now and turning over in her grave. Which would have outraged her more? he wondered. Israel's refusal to let me enter this country, or my rejection of her faith?

Finally, an officer approached him and asked in American accent, "Did you sign any petitions last year?" From the way he spoke, Jeremiah guessed that he too was from New York City.

During his university years and afterwards, while everyone around him was protesting and waving placards, Jeremiah kept a low profile on political matters. He preferred to save his public passion for brewing coffee. Yet, while he was living in Oakland, he had signed a petition organized by Jewish Voice for Peace to pressure his local grocery store to join an international boycott of settlement goods from Israel.

After the store agreed to stop importing such goods, the petition went viral. It collected hundreds of thousands of signatures within a few days, and initiated a nation-wide campaign directed at grocery stores across the United States. As the first petition to advocate the Boycott, Divestment, and Sanctions movement—soon to be known by the acronym BDS—and to be signed by thousands of Americans, it was reported on widely within the US and beyond. The petition called out by name the most aggressively anti-Palestinian groups and warned activists that lawsuits might be used to silence them. *The Times of*

Israel ran a story, in English, Arabic, Chinese, and Hebrew, comparing the boycott to the Nazi boycott of Jewish goods. *The Algeimeiner* ran an op-ed that described boycotts as the worst form of antisemitism because they failed to respect the right to self-determination of the world's only Jewish state.

As one of the first to sign, Jeremiah's name was near the top of the list. Anyone who clicked on the petition immediately came across his name as soon as they started scrolling down the list of signatories. Jeremiah knew that he was publicly on record as a BDS supporter. The year prior, the Knesset had passed the Entry into Israel Law, making it unlawful for any boycott supporter to enter Israel. He had heard the news but didn't dream that the airport guards would be following the politics around a local New York City grocery store.

Jeremiah figured out what was going on as soon as the officer asked him whether he had signed any petitions. He was shown a screenshot of the petition with his name near the top and asked to confirm whether that was him.

"What makes it illegal to support a boycott of settlement goods when the settlements are themselves illegal under international law?" Jeremiah asked the officer.

He recalled that Stefan had disputed the Entry into Israel Law when it was passed by the Knesset in 2017, but he assumed the guard would not be interested in the fine points of legal adjudication. He did not expect an answer, or at least not an intelligible one, but he had to ask nonetheless. For his conscience's sake.

"It's not our job to ask questions," the officer said. "Our job is to follow orders."

"So spoke the Nazi executioners," Jeremiah muttered

under his breath, softly enough so that the guard could not hear. He did not want to make his departure any more dramatic than it already was. He imagined his mother, turning over in her grave.

"Did you say something to me?" the officer asked.

"No," Jeremiah said flatly.

"Good. You're boarding the next plane out of here. The 12:30 flight to Amsterdam."

"What about Stefan?"

The officer's face was blank. "Who is Stefan."

"My companion," Jeremiah explained.

"What about him?" the officer said.

"Will he be flying with me?"

"That's up to him. If he does, he'll have to pay his own fare."

"Can I ask him?"

The officer stared at him for some time, trying to think of a reason to refuse the request. Eventually he gave up. "Okay," he said. "Wait a minute."

The guard returned five minutes later, with Stefan accompanying him. Never had the sight of another face relieved him so much. He had feared that he would have to fly back alone. Without thinking twice, he embraced his companion.

"I thought I'd have to fly back alone," Jeremiah whispered in Stefan's ear.

"You think I'd stay here without you?"

The guard stared at them menacingly. "No chit-chat until you're on board the flight."

Since they could not talk, they held hands while waiting in the detention room. Jeremiah caught the eye of a Sudanese baby, who stared back at him with intense curiosity, as if he had never seen someone who looked like him before. Hoping to keep the baby's attention, he began blinking. He and the baby traded glances until the baby burst into a smile.

The guards told them to stand as soon as the plane began taxiing towards the terminal. They refused to make eye contact with Jeremiah and ignored him when he held out his hand. Stefan didn't even bother looking back. At that moment, Jeremiah too wondered why he had bothered to try to make friends with anyone in Israel. Was it because of his mother that he retained a sentimental attachment to the country that she had always looked on as her protection in a world that harbored deep hatred towards Jews? Perhaps, he reflected, the time had arrived to cut his ties with this sentimentality. After all, his mother was dead. Time to start a life of his own, a life that rejected apartheid in full.

As they settled in their seats, Stefan took Jeremiah's hand again in his own. The last time he had held anyone else's hand for as long as he had held Stefan's that day was when his mother picked up him up from nursery school back in Brooklyn. This time it felt different, as if he was beginning a new life rather than trying to escape from an old one. He gripped Stefan's fingers as the plane took off. They seemed to give him strength.

"I was so worried while waiting for you," Stefan whispered. "I worried they would hurt you. Are you ok?"

Jeremiah gipped his hand more tightly as Stefan repeated, "Are you ok?"

Acknowledgements

The quotations from Ibn Arabi are taken from the translation of Michael Sells (*The Translator of Desires: Poems* [Princeton University Press, 2021]), at p. 11 and 19-21. respectively.

These stories have appeared in earlier versions in the following publications:

"Hands," was selected by Seren Books as their Short Story of the Month (July 2019).

"Speaking in Tongues," *Lovers' Lies*, ed. Katy Darby and Cherry Potts (London: Arachne Press, 2013), 85-91. The version presented here is heavily revised.

"The Breakdown of Love," *The Scores: A Journal of Poetry and Prose* 3 (2018).

"Like a Cavafy Poem" was awarded the New Zealand Flash Fiction prize in 2019 and subsequently appeared in *Cobalt*.

Thanks to my beloved family Kate Gould, Beth Gould, Brenda Gould. To Kayvan Tahmasebian for his integrity, his brilliance, and his critical reading. To Saleh Razzouk for giving life to these stories in Arabic, and Laith al-Hajjan who published them.

To the Study Hall Creative Critique Group: Elizabeth Lash, Sophie Gertrude Strohmeier, Nora Maynard, Molly Quell, Michael Friedrich, and Jodi Hausen, and other members who have engaged with my work.

THE AUTHOR

Rebecca Ruth Gould is a writer and translator based in the UK. Her most recent book is *Erasing Palestine* (Verso, 2023). Her translations from Persian with Kayvan Tahmasebian have received PEN Presents and PEN Translates awards from English PEN. She is currently working on a book entitled *Doves Born from Light: Writers' Homes and Readers' Lives* and an oral history of the Gaza Genocide with the Lighthouse Collective. She writes and edits *The Textual Materialist* newsletter and is Distinguished Professor of Comparative Poetics and Global Politics, School of Oriental and African Studies, University of London.

www.ingramcontent.com/pod-product-compliance
Lightning Source LLC
Chambersburg PA
CBHW021728190726
48288CB00009B/2950